KITTY TWEDDLE
AND THE WISHING WELL

H.J. BLENKINSOP

www.hjblenkinsop.com

ISBN-10: 1522961631
ISBN-13: 978-1522961635

For Helen and David.

ACKNOWLEDGMENTS

If it were not for the support of my fellow writer, blogger and critique partner, Sarah Dernley, this book simply wouldn't exist. Her unending support and attention to detail have been invaluable. A massive thanks Sarah! My sister Lorna has been a huge encouragement and my very first reader. I am also extremely fortunate that my partner in life Andrew gives me all the time in the world to write. Finally, a huge thank you to Helen and David, who told me about the well...

1 THE BINDING

"IT'S UNNATURAL," said Beatrice Witcher as she stared into the storm. Rain hammered against the window panes and the wind rattled through the house, whipping through the old woman's gray hair. She stood with her hands on her hips, glaring at the night while red curtains billowed around her.

Behind her, a young woman cried out in agony.

Beatrice spun around and rushed to the bed to examine her patient. "Not long to go now, Sarah. Breathe, breathe, in and out, in and out." She held Sarah's hand tight and pushed the sweat streaked brown hair away from Sarah's freckled brow.

Suddenly, the lights flickered and went out.

The storm lashed against the window like a whip. Tree branches scratched at the glass like dead fingers trying to pry their way in. The crack of thunder was deafening. Lightning followed in a flash, illuminating the dark shadow of a man outside.

Beatrice's head snapped up and she scowled. "He knows."

She got up, walked to the window and closed the curtains with a dramatic swish of her arms. What little light filtered in between each lightning flash vanished. In complete darkness, Beatrice reached for a candle and lit it with a match. She didn't need to see them, she knew exactly where they were. She suspected this might happen and came prepared. A witch is always prepared.

"What's happening? Who's here?" gasped Sarah.

"Nothing for you to worry about," said Beatrice. She set the candle down on the nightstand and smiled, making the corners of her eyes crinkle. Beatrice mopped Sarah's brow and said, "You have more important work to do."

Someone knocked on the door before opening it. "I came as quickly as I could," said a balding man in a tweed jacket, setting down a black leather bag.

"Dr. McKracken, you're just in time."

The baby took its first breath and let out a healthy cry.

"You're lucky, it's a girl." Beatrice beamed when the doctor handed the bundled up baby to her mother.

Beatrice noted the time on the clock. It was just after midnight. Beatrice knew what this meant. Any child born after midnight on a Friday, but before sunrise on Saturday, is gifted with the power to see the fey folk. If she's powerful, and knowing who the father was, she would be, the child may even be able to enter Fairyland.

"A very healthy baby, congratulations." The doctor smiled and then exchanged glances with Beatrice.

The witch chose her next words carefully. She didn't want to frighten the new mother. "Your daughter is very special," she crooned. "She has… gifts."

"What kind of gifts?"

"Magical gifts. Powerful gifts," the witch whispered. "Gifts that, for your daughter's own protection, must be hidden. To keep her safe," she added quickly. "I must bind her powers until she is old enough to understand them."

Sarah looked from Dr. McKracken to Beatrice and nodded in understanding. "Will it hurt her?"

"Not at all," Beatrice answered honestly. "I am sure the good doctor won't mind staying an extra few moments for reassurance?"

"Of course I'll stay. I assure you, your daughter is in good hands," said Dr. McKracken. "I've known Beatrice all my life." He nodded toward the witch.

"But first," Beatrice said, "she needs a name. A powerful name, a name that will offer her protection."

"I've already chosen one." Sarah's face lit up.

The witch held up a finger in warning. "Remember, words have power and names are the most powerful words there are."

"I know," the young woman said, nodding. "And places have power too."

"Yes, they do." Beatrice raised her eyebrows in surprise. Perhaps Sarah was better prepared to take care of a magical child than she expected.

"This house is built on the grounds of an old convent," Sarah began. "It's consecrated ground, which means it's protected." She paused to kiss her baby on the forehead. "The first Mother Superior was called Katherine. I'd like to name my daughter after her."

The witch nodded and said, "Yes, I think that will do nicely." She looked at the baby and smiled.

"But I'd like to shorten it," Sarah said, "to Kitty."

Beatrice nodded in approval. "Hand the baby over to me, the binding ritual will only take a moment."

The baby snuffled at the blanket, a tuft of dark brown hair poked out. While thunder growled outside, Beatrice cradled the child in her arms, muttering words and making symbols over the baby's head. Reaching for a small silver bottle covered in strange runes, she unstopped the cork with her teeth and poured a few drops onto the baby's forehead.

"It's done." Beatrice rocked the baby gently. "Listen very carefully. I have bound her powers so that those who would harm her cannot detect her. It also means she cannot use them and will not know she has magic at all. The binding will wear off on her twelfth birthday. You must bring her back to me, here in the village of Dribble, before then, so that I can teach her how to use them. Do you understand?"

Sarah nodded.

"Do you promise?" Beatrice asked seriously.

"Yes, I promise."

"Only I can train her. It is imperative that I teach her how to use her magic before the binding unravels."

The sounds of the storm outside began to fade. The thunder grumbled further away and the lightning took longer to strike. The rain pitter-pattered before stopping completely. It seemed the storm had blown itself out.

Dr. McKracken got up, walked to the bedroom door and poked his head out. "Victor, Sally, may I present your granddaughter, Kitty Tweddle."

Victor and Sally Tweddle rushed into the room, anxious to see their daughter and grandchild. Freckles spread over Sally's smiling face. She looked just like her daughter, they even had the same hazel eyes. Victor pushed back his mop of sandy blond hair, graying at the temples, to hold up his camera and take a photograph of Beatrice holding the baby.

"I'll be back tomorrow to check on mother and child," said Dr. McKracken, picking up his black bag and pulling his scarf around his neck before leaving the room.

Beatrice carefully handed little Kitty back to her mother and then wrapped her shawl around her shoulders. "I'll also be back tomorrow to check on Kitty and Sarah," she said as she left. She stopped at the door and looked back. Mother and grandparents surrounded the child. Three generations of Tweddles together. Good, she thought, little Kitty will need all the help she can get.

Closing the front door of number five Crescent Avenue behind her, Beatrice stepped out into a dark and soggy night. Although the rain had stopped, little rivulets ran along the gutters before disappearing down the drains. An old streetlight spilled white light onto a puddle outside the front gate. Beatrice hopped over it and began the short walk home through the village of Dribble, passing the library and the little cemetery behind it.

The sound of her boots echoed along the tree-lined streets. She pulled her house keys out of her pocket. Not a leaf moved. Not a creature stirred. A prickly feeling ran down her spine. She cast her senses out. Even the little rivulets of rainwater run-off had stopped.

As she walked, she heard another set of footsteps behind her.

The prickly feeling exploded and every sense screamed *danger!*

The footsteps behind her changed from the clop of boots to the patter of paws.

She took a deep breath and summoned all of her power, imagining it well up inside her like a million stars that only she could see.

The owner of the paws was getting closer, and those paws had claws that scratched along the wet ground, loud in the eerie silence.

Her breath quickening, Beatrice channeled her power from a sparkling ball in her chest, down her arms and into her hands where it tingled unseen at her fingertips.

Ragged breath from the thing behind was so close it made her shiver.

She had to act now. Gathering her resolve, she spun around to face her stalker, hands raised up, ready to release her magic.

Too late.

The creature struck before she could utter a word.

The next morning, police found Beatrice Witcher's house keys lying on the ground—in a pool of her own blood.

2 THE FORBIDDEN ROOM

Almost twelve years later in present day Scotland.

"THE NEXT TRAIN arriving at platform two will be the 11.05am to London Kings Cross," a female voice crackled over the loudspeaker. Pigeons flew above while hundreds of people scuttled around like ants below them. The old train station was a mass of iron girders that arched high overhead like the ribs of a long-dead beast.

Kitty Tweddle stared at the huge boards listing departure and arrival times as they flickered and changed all at once. Usually, she would have found a train station an exciting place to be. It would mean she was going on a trip, an adventure somewhere amazing.

Only she wasn't.

"Come along darling, please hurry, I need to be on that train," Kitty's mother pleaded, half dragging her through the busy Edinburgh train station. With Sarah Tweddle's pale freckled hand clasped around her daughter's tawny wrist, they trudged not toward platform two and the train to London, but toward the taxi rank.

I, not we, thought Kitty. A torrent of dark brown hair flopped over her downcast face as she lugged her suitcase behind her. "But mum, I don't want to spend the summer with Grandma and Grandpa, I want to spend the summer with my friends!"

Her mother said nothing and continued to drag her along which made Kitty feel childish. She was almost twelve after all.

She did want to spend the summer holidays with her friends—more than anything. Days at the beach, evenings in the park, and the Rising Sun Festival, everyone would be there. But now it was ruined. Worse than ruined, because her friends were going to have the best summer ever and she wouldn't be there.

A black taxicab idled at the rank and the driver jumped out to help Kitty with her suitcase. Her mother opened the door and bundled Kitty inside. "I'm so sorry darling, I truly am, but you know I have to work."

Her mother's job with a marketing company was taking her to India after a brief stop off in London. So while her mother would spend her free time riding elephants and eating spicy food, Kitty would be stuck in a Scottish village with her grandparents for the whole summer.

Kitty quickly kissed her mother goodbye, the cab door slammed shut, and the engine spluttered to life in an instant. Kitty turned to wave goodbye, but her mother had already turned her back and was rushing away toward platform two. Kitty watched her disappear into the crowd while the taxi drove away.

She felt numb as the taxi emerged from the underground station and turned left onto the bridge crossing Princes Street Gardens.

"I don't get many fares to the village of Dribble," said the taxi driver. "Staying with family are you?"

"Yes," Kitty grunted.

She barely noticed the gothic Scott Monument looming darkly ahead of her, or the narrow winding stairways that disappeared up and down the shadowy alleys off Market Street. The only thing Kitty did notice is that it had stopped raining. It had been raining forever and the gloomy sky above promised more rain to come.

"Not being from around here, you won't have heard about the missing gargoyles then?" the taxi driver said. "Several of them have disappeared over the last couple of weeks. It's been all over the news."

"Oh?" Kitty mumbled.

The taxi stopped at a traffic light by an old church, the kind with little statues and lots of fancy carved stone. Only bits of the stone were broken off in places and several of the little statues were gone, leaving empty niches in the walls like sightless eyes.

Kitty looked up at the church's weather-worn surface, taking in the dirt-blackened stone. Her eyes settled on the faces of two gargoyles sticking out from the walls like enormous ears. One had a beak like an eagle while the other had a dragon's snout. Both were long and lean with wings carved the length of their bodies. Their heads were splattered with pigeon poop.

Kitty blinked back a tear. This really was going to be the worst summer ever. With a sigh, she let her head press against the window, then jumped when one of the gargoyles turned its head, its stony eyes looking right at her. Kitty rubbed her eyes furiously. When her vision cleared, the gargoyles were back the way they had been, staring straight ahead.

Did I really see them move? Kitty thought. The traffic lights turned green and the taxi pulled away.

The gargoyles took off in pursuit of Kitty's taxi, catching up fast. They glanced at each other in mid-flight, grim determination etched on their stony faces as they swooped down toward the vehicle.

The taxi driver caught sight of a blur in his rear view mirror. "What the…"

Kitty twisted about in the back seat, trying to look out of the window. She caught a glimpse of something dark and flapping but then the taxi swerved. The driver swore and Kitty fell to one side, losing sight of the dark things chasing them. When she regained her balance and looked again, she couldn't see them.

Above, the gargoyles opened their muzzles to screech in warning. In a flash, they vanished, their screams snatched from the air with them.

The taxi driver shook his head and mumbled something under his breath. Kitty was turned around in the back seat, scanning the sky. Whatever she had seen was gone. Moving around to face the front, she adjusted her seat belt and sighed.

It was a short ride to her grandparents' house which was only two miles from the train station. They lived on a tree-lined street with beautiful gardens filled with large and exotic plants. Enormous shrubs covered in candy-floss pink flowers peeked over garden walls, while purple trumpet shaped flowers climbed the gates.

Kitty got out of the taxi and looked around, the smell of flowers filling her nostrils. Each Georgian house stood proudly among the tree-line. Many were modest gray stone buildings like her grandparents' house. Others were huge mansions bearing turrets or clock towers that jutted out from the leafy canopy making it look like an overgrown gothic city.

The taxi drove away leaving Kitty standing alone on the pavement with her suitcase outside number five, Crescent Avenue.

"Kitty, my love!" her Grandma, a slender woman wearing over sized gardening gloves, called from the front garden. Waving feverishly with a trowel, she hurried down the path, the breeze blowing her streaked chestnut hair away from a broad forehead. "We're so delighted to have you spend the summer with us," she said, tears welling in her hazel eyes, her smile so wide it made her chin look pointy. As she reached the front gate, she flung out her arms and hugged Kitty.

Over her Grandma's shoulder, Kitty spotted Grandpa waving from the front door, his broad shouldered, six-foot frame filling it. His shock of white hair stood out against the red painted door.

Kitty had not been inside her grandparents' house since she was a little girl and couldn't remember much about it. She entered the house and saw a towering grandfather clock, wood-paneled walls, and a huge stuffed fish mounted on the wall. One set of stairs wound up several floors while another set wound down toward a glass door. Light flooded into the hallway through a skylight three floors up.

The clock chimed eleven times.

"Oh dear," said Grandpa looking at his watch. "I'll need to wind the clock—it's running almost ten minutes slow again." He turned to a small wooden cabinet next to the clock and unhinged the clasp. Upon several rows of hooks hung keys of every kind. From ordinary front door keys to tiny silver keys, the use for which Kitty could not guess, to long heavy iron keys that looked extremely old. Old enough to unlock a castle drawbridge or a dungeon grate, she supposed.

Grandpa's bushy white eyebrows knitted together. Finally, he selected a medium-sized brass key with a hollow end from the cabinet. He wound up the clock. It chimed thirteen times.

Kitty looked up the stairs. "Where will my room be?"

"Not up there," said Grandpa, "down here." He gestured toward the stairs that disappeared down to the glass door below. On the door was a small plaque which read, *5 ½ Crescent Avenue*. "We usually rent out the basement apartment to students, but our student has gone home for the summer so we thought you might like it." He smiled crookedly. "Would you like your own apartment for the summer, Kitty?"

"Oh yes!" Kitty gasped, unable to believe it. Could this be possible? Could her grandparents be giving her an apartment for the summer? Things had just gotten a whole lot better.

The apartment was not separate from the house, but it had its own bedroom, bathroom and small kitchen—and its own address.

"Aren't you going to let Kitty have some tea and cake before showing her around?" asked Grandma.

"I think Kitty wants to see the basement," Grandpa said with a smile. "We'll be back upstairs in just a moment."

Kitty followed Grandpa, pulling her suitcase behind her.

Bumping her suitcase down the stone steps to the basement, she passed an enormous oil painting of a ship in a storm that was big enough to swallow her whole.

It was cooler down in the basement. And darker. It also smelled slightly musty, like a strange mixture of old books and chipped stone with a bit of moss thrown in for luck.

She jerked away from the item hanging at the foot of the stairs. A long-handled axe. The kind a woodcutter would use.

It looked sharp and dangerous.

"Here's your room," Grandpa said, interrupting her thoughts. He opened up a door to a small room with a low ceiling. "Just as well you're not too tall."

Kitty hurried along the corridor to join him.

It was the kind of bedroom Kitty expected to find in a castle.

Elegantly furnished with a four-poster bed, polished wooden desk and a small red easy chair next to a stone corner fireplace. A large tapestry in golds and reds covered the wall next to it.

"The bathroom is back toward the stairs, across the hall is a tiny kitchen and this door here." He knocked on a wooden door on the outside wall. "Leads into the garden. Just remember to keep it locked at night."

He reached into his jacket pocket and pulled out a long key with an intricate handle and handed it to Kitty. "Just leave the key in the lock after you use it."

Kitty took the key, rolling it around in her hands. It was at least six inches long and forged of dark metal. She slipped it into her pocket.

"Oh, and this might come in handy too." He handed her a keyring. "That's an LED flashlight," he said with a nod.

"Thanks," said Kitty switching the tiny flashlight on and shining its blue-white beam up and down the hallway. The light shone on doors opening up to the other rooms, but the door at the very back, nearest the stairs, got her attention.

"What's in there?" Kitty asked, shining the light on the door. It was red paneled with a rusty padlock.

"Ah." Grandpa chuckled. "This is the one room you must never enter," he said as he rattled the padlock on the door.

Before Kitty could ask why, Grandpa said, "I'll let you get settled in." Then he disappeared up the stone staircase calling out behind him, "Grandma baked, so come upstairs for some tea and ginger cake when you're ready."

Kitty gave the locked door one last look. She'd just arrived and already there was a place she was forbidden to enter. "Hmm..." Kitty mulled over what secrets could be concealed there.

She stuffed her hands into her pockets and felt the key.

Turning around, she placed key in the lock. It turned with a satisfying click. She twisted the handle and pulled it open.

Outside the rain bounced like pinballs off a rose bush climbing around the back door, shredding the rose petals into soggy piles.

She looked out onto a walled garden. At the bottom of the garden was an old plum tree. The tree trunk twisted like a wrung out dishcloth and green leaves hung heavy on the ends of its elderly branches.

It was dark under the twisted plum tree. Too dark to see the owner of two yellow eyes peering out from the shadows. Kitty Tweddle didn't know it, but she was being watched.

3 SHADOWS IN THE NIGHT

THE SKY GREW DARKER and the rain strummed heavily, drawing moths and daddy longlegs toward the light spilling from the open back door. Time to close it, Kitty thought, while she checked carefully around the frame, removing the snails that had slimed their way almost to the top at a remarkable speed.

One especially fat snail refused to move. She pulled at its shell and then stopped, more than a little horrified at how well it had welded itself to the doorframe.

Grabbing a soup spoon from the tiny kitchen across the hall, she eased the fat snail away using the handle end. It recoiled at the touch of metal and she placed it gently down in a sodden flowerbed under the kitchen window.

Turning her attention to the next snail, Kitty gasped when the soup spoon tugged itself free of her hand and hovered in the air in front of her. She stared in open-mouthed surprise when it spun around like a windmill before tapping each of the three remaining snails on their shells, all by itself.

Kitty jumped back as one by one, the snails shot across the garden, landing safely on the wet lawn. Its job done, the spoon dropped to the ground with a clatter. "What?" Kitty was speechless. How could the spoon do all of that on its own?

Carefully, she picked up the spoon and examined it. It looked quite ordinary.

"Hmm..." Her brow crinkled, trying to understand what had just happened.

Walking back to the tiny kitchen, she tossed the spoon into the sink. That's when she heard a sound behind her.

Flop, flop, splat.

Returning to the door, she gasped in surprise. There, two feet inside her basement, was a... thing. Dark green and slimy with long glistening toes and black beady eyes, it was about the size of a fist. It must be a frog, she reasoned, it looked quite froggy. But this frog had an altogether lumpy, or more accurately, warty back. Ah, a toad.

She tried to shoo it away, but the toad stood its ground. She picked up a polka dot umbrella that was hanging on the back of the kitchen door and poked it at the toad. The toad rolled its beady eyes.

"Excuse me," said the toad, glaring at her.

Shocked, Kitty opened the umbrella in the toad's face. The toad jumped back in surprise.

"Be careful what you wish for!" the toad warned dramatically before flopping away into the garden, leaving toad-shaped splatter marks on the floor.

Kitty slammed the door shut and leaned against it, the umbrella still in her hand. Her heart was pounding.

I didn't wish for anything.

"Kitty?" Grandpa called down the stairs. "Are you coming to join us for some tea and cake? The kettle is almost boiled."

"Just a minute!" Kitty turned and locked the back door

with the iron key, making sure to leave it securely in the lock, as her Grandpa had instructed. Taking a deep breath, she headed upstairs. Walking into the kitchen, her nostrils filled with the smell of ginger cake.

"Fresh out of the oven," said Grandma stooped over the old stove making tea. The kettle whistled to a boil. The kitchen was old fashioned with wooden floors and a wooden dresser in one corner lined with china cups and plates. It stood opposite a large bay window, flanked by red curtains.

"Here you are dear, only a little slice. It won't be long until dinner." Grandma brought the ginger cake to the table and cut Kitty a square with an enormous knife.

Kitty slumped into a spindle-backed chair and ate her ginger cake hungrily.

The rain hammered down on the window followed by a flash of lightning.

Kitty flinched and then counted in her head, one elephant, two elephants, three elephants, four elephants, five elephants, before a crack of thunder rumbled around the house. "The center of the storm must be five miles away," she said. She had heard somewhere that counting elephants between the flashes of lightning and the crunch of thunder, told you how many miles away the center of the storm was.

"It's good to be inside on a day like today, isn't it?" said Grandpa, lifting the teapot toward her. He poured tea into a china teacup. "Milk?"

Lightning forked outside the window again, lighting up the whole sky for a split second. Kitty counted again, one elephant, two elephants, three elephants—

CRACK!

The thunder boomed like splitting wood, so loud that it shook the whole house. The tea danced in Kitty's cup and on the mantle above the stove, Grandma's china teddy bears wobbled.

The rain pelted against the windows like hammers. It was so ferocious, Kitty thought the windows might break, or the roof might be ripped off, or the house might be shaken from its granite foundation.

FLASH!

For a split second, the dark silhouette of a person was outlined in the window.

Kitty screamed.

CRACK!

Grandma dropped her teacup and it smashed on the floor, scattering pieces of white china around a puddle of milky tea.

"There's someone at the window," Kitty's voice shook. She jumped up and grabbed her Grandpa's hand.

"Nonsense," said Grandpa. He gently guided Kitty back to her chair and walked toward the window. He stood in front of it, drawn up to his full height of six feet two with his hands on his hips as if daring the dark form to reappear. It did not.

"Just a trick of the light," he reassured. "Lightning can make us think we see things that are not there," he continued, drawing the red curtains closed. "We don't believe in magic and superstition in this house."

The lightning flared through the curtains making the whole room flash crimson. The thunder that followed set the entire room shaking once again. Grandpa stood in front of the window like a guardian, prepared to stop anything from coming in. Or at least that's what Kitty imagined.

Grandma stirred a simmering pot on the stove. Delicious smells drifted across the kitchen. "The stew is almost done."

Kitty's tummy growled when Grandma set a steaming bowl of stew in front of her. As she ate, the storm began to ease. The lightning was dimmer, the elephant count longer, and the thunder quieter.

She had barely finished her bowl of stew when another bowl filled with plum cobbler, topped with rich vanilla ice cream, arrived in its place. The ice cream melted and ran down the sides of the crispy topping while steam twisted away and disappeared.

"The plums are from our tree at the bottom of the garden," Grandma said with pride.

Even though she was quite full, Kitty picked up her spoon and plunged in. It was delicious. She scraped the bowl clean and flopped back in her chair knowing she couldn't eat another bite.

"Well, after today's excitement perhaps an early night is in order," said Grandpa, standing up to clear the table. "Kitty you must be exhausted after your journey today."

Kitty had to admit, she was tired now that she thought about it. Kissing her grandparents good night, she slipped down the stone stairs into her basement. She expected it would take ages to fall asleep in a strange bed, but her head was barely on the pillow before she drifted off.

She woke up with a start to the sound of footsteps walking down the hallway. A shadow blocked out the thin band of light that shone under her bedroom door. Someone shook the handle on the back door and satisfied it was locked, walked away again. Kitty closed her eyes and then opened them abruptly when she heard the chains on the forbidden room rattle and someone turn the key in the padlock.

"Oh no!" Grandpa's voice carried down the hallway.

Kitty heard him walk back up the stairs before sliding out of bed and creeping to her bedroom door. Looking along the basement hallway, she could see that Grandpa was gone, but the door to the forbidden room stood ajar. She strained her eyes, but it was too dark to see inside.

Tiptoeing along the hallway, she peered inside the red door to the forbidden room to get a better look. Light from the hallway glimmered off the dark stone floor. Kitty squinted, it looked like a big puddle.

Hearing Grandpa's footsteps coming back down the stairs, she darted along the hallway and into her room. Jumping back into bed, she pulled the covers right up to her chin and lay there, listening. She heard clanking and perhaps some scraping but could not out figure out what the sounds were.

Finally, all fell silent and Kitty fell back to sleep, this time until morning.

Nutmeg watched from beneath the plum tree at the bottom of the garden. It was still raining. His yellow eyes narrowed in disgust when a huge raindrop made its way through the plumy canopy and dropped onto his head. Like most cats, he did not like the rain. Absentmindedly, he licked a paw and began grooming his bushy ginger fur—all without taking his eyes off the back door of 5 ½ Crescent Avenue.

"Hmm," he snorted triumphantly. "A wishing well toad." He was right all along. Something bad and definitely magical was intruding into this world. And it was coming in through that basement. Things were about to get out of hand. He turned and began to sharpen his claws on the twisted trunk of the plum tree. He'd better be ready.

When all the lights in the house went out, he left his watch post under the tree and went off in search of his friends. It didn't take him long to find Baby, a beautiful Siamese cat with a beige coat, chocolate brown facial markings and turquoise eyes.

"Baby! Baby!" Nutmeg hissed, diving underneath the eaves where Baby was sheltering. "I was right, something bad is happening at 5 ½ Crescent Avenue."

Baby licked a paw and washed her face. She licked it again and slicked it over her left ear. "Just slow down," she said, stopping to look at Nutmeg. "What's happening and how do you know?"

Nutmeg told her what he had seen, from the new human to the wishing well toad's cryptic warning.

"What?" Baby stopped her grooming. "The human actually heard the toad speak?"

"Yes."

"She understood what it said?"

"Perfectly."

"What did she do?"

"She shooed it away with a polka dot umbrella and slammed the door shut behind her."

"Hmm..." Baby considered this carefully. If she was a witch she would not have been so rude to the toad. Baby mulled over the possibilities. "Either she is a bad tempered witch or ... or..."

"Or what?" Nutmeg asked, wide eyed.

"Or she doesn't know she's a witch." Baby looked out at the rain. "Do you think she is aware of the danger she is in?"

"Probably not. She seems quite, you know, young."

"We have to warn her."

"What?" Nutmeg gasped. "Talk to a human?" He shook his head. "Is that really wise?"

"If she could hear and understand the wishing well toad speak, she is far from ordinary," Baby said, still staring out into the rain. "We have to warn her and help her if we can. If she has moved into 5 ½ Crescent Avenue, she is in danger."

4 THE WALLED GARDEN

KITTY AWOKE, pulled back the bed covers and felt a damp chill wrap around her legs. Pulling the long curtains wide, she wiped condensation off the old windows to peer outside. Everything looked soggy and gloomy, but at least the rain had stopped.

She put on her slippers and dressing gown. Walking along the basement hallway she paused at the door to the forbidden room, only long enough to see it was padlocked once more. She touched the padlock lightly and goosebumps prickled over her arms. Letting go, she glanced at the axe hanging on the wall before running up the spiral staircase and into the kitchen.

The smell of toast filled the room.

"Oh, you're awake." Grandpa turned the page on his newspaper.

"Did you sleep well, love?" Grandma asked. She brought over a cup and saucer and without waiting for an answer said, "There's tea in the pot."

"What are you going to do today?" Grandpa asked.

"Dunno. Explore the garden... maybe..." Kitty poured

herself some tea and grabbed a slice toast from the rack in front of her, nibbling on it dry.

"You might want to see what Marcus and Emily are up to," said Grandma. "They live next door."

"And she might not." Grandpa's voice arose from somewhere within his newspaper.

"Oh shoosh," Grandma scolded him. Picking up a tea towel she began drying dishes. "And if you happen to speak with our other neighbor, Dr. McKracken, take whatever he says with a pinch of salt." Grandma scoured the cup she was drying before turning around and whispering, "He's mad as a bag of squirrels that one."

The newspaper in front of Grandpa quivered with what might have been a chuckle. "She might find Dr. McKracken more fun than Marcus and Emily."

Kitty giggled and turned to see Grandma open what appeared to be a cupboard door in the corner of the room. She disappeared only to reappear a few moments later through the main door carrying fresh tea towels.

"How did you do that? I mean where does it lead—I thought it was a cupboard," Kitty spluttered.

Grandma smiled. "This house is full of surprises."

She put the tea towels into the draw and turned back to face Kitty. "It is a cupboard, a shared cupboard between two rooms. Quite typical in older Scottish homes. So, you can walk into it in the kitchen, and walk out into the dining room. Come on, I'll show you."

Kitty dashed over to the cupboard door and flung it open. It was dark, but enough light filtered in from the kitchen to reveal its 'S' shape. It was lined with shelves crammed with old candlesticks, vases, boxes, and books. More boxes littered the floor. Kitty started to wind her way around them.

Grandma flipped a switch and an orange light flickered, making the cupboard even spookier. "See, just a cupboard."

Kitty popped out into the dining room and closed the door behind her.

"Come and finish your breakfast, you've hardly eaten a bite," Grandma's voice traveled through the cupboard.

Kitty was fast growing to love her grandparents' house. With a whole apartment to herself downstairs and secret passages (at least, she thought the cupboard counted as a secret passage) she realized this summer might not be so bad after all. She made her way back to the kitchen table and picked up her toast.

"When we bought this house we were told about another passageway," Grandpa said from behind his newspaper.

"Where?" asked Kitty.

"Oh, that's right." Grandma nodded. "The story goes that this house was built by two brothers who were rather thrifty and shared a butler. By building a semi-attached house, that means two houses joined together, they each got a home of their own but by building a doorway between the two houses, the butler could go between."

"Where is this passageway?" Kitty was on the edge of her seat.

"Oh, we've never found it," said Grandma with a chuckle.

"If there ever was one," said Grandpa.

"Just another story..." Grandma's voice trailed off as she stirred her tea.

After breakfast, Kitty dressed and walked into the small front garden, facing out onto Crescent Avenue.

"Goodness, Judith, look at the state of your lawn."

Kitty heard a very snooty voice speaking louder than necessary from across the street. Walking to the garden gate, she saw that the voice came from a severe looking woman, tall and lean with black bobbed hair. She was peering into a neighbor's garden.

"I do hope you will do a little light gardening and ahem..." The snooty woman waved her hand around. "Clean it up. We have standards to uphold on this street." She sniffed, sticking her nose into the air.

Kitty heard the sound of an approaching car. "Good morning Mrs. Snodgrass," said a man in a green sports car as he slowed to a stop.

Kitty couldn't quite see his face, but he had dark shaggy hair and a friendly voice. His car, while in perfect condition, looked very old.

"Oh, Mr. Wolf." Mrs. Snodgrass turned to face him, suddenly all smiles. Her demeanor had changed completely. "My what a beautiful car," she said and then giggled, running her hand along the side.

"It's a 1972 Porsche 911. Chartreuse with black leather interior." Mr. Wolf beamed. "She is a beauty isn't she?"

"Yes..." Mrs. Snodgrass ran her finger over a polished silver wing mirror. "Delightful."

"I'm so glad I caught you, Mrs. Snodgrass." Mr. Wolf cleared his throat. "We are short staffed at the library this evening—it's our late night—and I was wondering if you could possibly cover?"

"Oh, I see," Mrs. Snodgrass replied with a weak smile.

"I know it's not your usual shift, but if you could help out, I would really appreciate it."

"Of course." Mrs. Snodgrass sighed.

"Fantastic. I'll see you at five o'clock."

The man turned right around to look at Kitty. "Hello!" He waved pleasantly. "You must be Kitty Tweddle?"

"Yes." Kitty supposed he must have seen her as he drove down the street.

"If you're looking for any reading material for the summer holidays, we have lots of wonderful books in our village library. I hope we'll see you soon?"

"Oh...um... yes?" Kitty stammered, not feeling able to say no. She had already brought plenty of books with her and Moby Dick was at the top of her reading list.

"Wonderful." He smiled from ear to ear and revved the engine. "See you soon, Kitty." He turned, nodded toward Mrs. Snodgrass and drove away.

Kitty watched his car disappear around the corner. He seemed friendly and much nicer than the snooty Mrs. Snodgrass who liked to tell people off about their gardens.

Mrs. Snodgrass's eyes narrowed, staring at Kitty. Her smiles had disappeared and her face twisted into an angry pout.

I hope she lives at the other end of the street, Kitty thought. She walked back to the house feeling Mrs. Snodgrass's eyes burrowing into her back.

She closed the front door and went straight down the stairs to the basement. Perhaps the back garden would be more fun.

The back door was even more difficult to open than the day before. Kitty tied a towel around the handle to give her extra leverage, leaned back and pulled with her whole body weight to get it to budge. It groaned and creaked open.

The rain had washed away the tattered pink petals from the day before. A pool of water stood where the drain should be and the middle of the lawn looked very boggy. Kitty stepped outside onto the damp flagstones and noticed a small white statue of a woman standing under an apple tree.

Further down the garden she saw a small summerhouse with a red peaked roof, its walls crawling with purple flowers.

"Our mother says you don't have a dad," a girl's voice squeaked over the wall.

"Emily, that's not nice," said a boy's voice.

Kitty looked over the wall to the right and into the faces of two mousy haired, freckled faced children grinning evilly. "You must be Marcus and Emily."

"Yes and—"

"So you've heard about us already, quite right too." Marcus cut his sister off. "I'm fourteen and my little sister here is ten. How old are you?"

"Eleven, almost twelve," said Kitty.

"But she doesn't have a dad," Emily hissed from behind the wall.

"You can come and play with us if you like," Marcus offered.

"We're playing lords and ladies. You can be my lady in waiting," said Emily.

"No thanks," said Kitty through gritted teeth.

"What else have you got to do?" Emily whined.

"Plenty." Kitty turned and stomped through the boggy grass toward the back of the garden. A rotten apple flew by narrowly missing her head, followed by a chorus of evil laughter. Kitty could feel the dampness of the waterlogged lawn seep through her shoes and socks, chilling her feet. Her throat felt tight, the way it did when she tried not to cry.

Kitty only had one memory of her father. He was standing in a doorway, his outline shadowed by the light spilling in from behind him. He leaned down toward her and said, "Silly girl." Turned around and left. The door closed behind him and he was gone. It was one of her earliest memories. She couldn't have been older than four. Kitty pressed her lips into a determined line and flared her nostrils, I'm not a silly girl!

"Chilly for June," said an elderly man.

That must be Dr. McKracken, thought Kitty. She took a breath before turning to face the direction of his gruff voice.

"I'd get out of that puddle you're standing in if I were you."

Kitty looked down and realized she'd sunk ever so slightly. Picking her way out of the puddle, she walked up to the wall Dr. McKracken was hanging over.

He looked like a skinny walrus, all jowls and whiskers with a bald head. He wore a tweed jacket over a shirt and tie. All of his clothes were in shades of brown.

"Nasty little creatures those two." He jerked his head in the direction the rotten apple had flown from. "But not as nasty as what's on the loose..."

Movement caught Kitty's eye and she saw two cats emerge from behind the plum tree, one ginger and one Siamese.

The Siamese stalked along the garden wall toward Kitty and Dr. McKracken. The ginger cat followed like a shadow.

Ignoring the cats, Kitty turned back to Dr. McKracken, "What do you mean?"

"What do I mean? I mean there's a bogeyman on the loose!" His eyes were wild. "Saw it last night I did. The lightning flashed in my kitchen window and there it was, his monstrous shadow filled up the whole window."

Kitty's eyes widened in shock.

"Ah, you saw it then?" Dr. McKracken nodded seeing the look of recognition in Kitty's face.

"Was it like the shadow of a man?" Kitty asked, remembering the dark shadow in the storm.

"Aye, but it's no man my dear, it's a bogeyman." He looked warily from side to side as if the bogeyman could be lurking nearby.

Kitty remembered what Grandma had said about Dr. McKracken, *mad as a bag of squirrels*. But what if he wasn't? What if he knew something?

"And then there's the strange case of the missing gargoyles, have you heard? Several of them have gone missing from buildings including two from St. Peter's, the old church on the corner."

Kitty remembered seeing them perched on the side of the old church while she was in the taxi coming from the train station. Her mind flooded with memories of the trip, of seeing their poop splattered heads, the traffic lights changing, the taxi swerving as dark shapes flew above and then disappeared. She needed to know more about what was really going on here.

"What is a bogeyman exactly and what does he want?" she asked.

Dr. McKracken sighed. "Forgive me, I didn't mean to scare you." He fumbled with what appeared to be a small magnifying glass in his hands.

"I'm not scared."

"No, no, of course you're not." He nodded, smiled and then looked through the small glass. "Marvelous, simply marvelous..." he muttered to himself.

Kitty knew he was trying change the subject.

He stopped peering through the small glass and glanced sideways at Kitty. "I wonder..." He came closer to the wall. "If you come a little bit down this way, close to the house, you'll see some of the stones on your side stick out, like steps."

Kitty followed the wall along and stood facing it. "I don't see any steps," she said.

"Keep looking."

"There's nothing here."

Dr. McKracken moved along the wall on the other side. "Stand right here, with your right ear to the wall and look toward the house."

Kitty did so. "Ah, I see them now."

"Sometimes you have to look at things from a different perspective to see what's right under your nose," he said.

Kitty climbed the worn steps, which were really just stones that stuck out from the wall, so that she was eye to eye with Dr. McKracken.

"Now then, take a peek through this and tell me what you see." He held the small looking-glass out to her.

Kitty took the glass and peered through it. "Whoa!" She almost dropped it.

Dr. McKracken nodded. "I knew this day would come," he said, looking appraisingly at Kitty. "Right from the moment you were born."

"What do you know about that?" Kitty stuttered, still shocked at what she had seen through the looking-glass.

"What do I know about your birth? Why Kitty Tweddle, I'm a doctor and I delivered you into this world. Didn't your grandparents tell you?"

Kitty shook her head.

"He appeared the night you were born too. Just like he appeared again last night. I knew this would happen. You'll be twelve in, what? A couple of weeks? Yes, that's why this is all happening..." He looked thoughtful and a bit far away.

Kitty gazed through the glass again. Everything sparkled. The moss growing between the cracks in the stone wall shone like gold. Peering closer, it moved like it was growing right before her eyes, stretching toward the light. Goosebumps crawled up her arms.

She glanced back at the garden and almost dropped the glass. "Wow." The white statue of a woman stirred and breathed, splashing water around her bathing pool. She looked up and noticed Kitty watching her and screamed, pulling a leaf from an overhanging apple tree to cover herself. "Sorry," mouthed Kitty, blushing.

Dr. McKracken scowled. "It's impolite to watch a lady bathing."

"Everything is... moving."

Turning the glass toward the plum tree at the bottom of the garden, Kitty watched as its trunk moved, its bark no longer dry and rough, but supple and glowing. The tree's gnarled limbs flexed like a hand, and its twigs unfurled like slender fingers and beckoned to her.

Kitty's breathing quickened.

She moved the glass along the wall at the bottom of the garden and stopped, lowering the glass to look above it. Her brow furrowed. "Curious..."

"What is it?" asked Dr. McKracken.

"I can see ripples of blue light, a sort of stream, flowing from the plum tree through the garden, but when I take the looking-glass away, it's gone."

"That's because what you're looking through is not a looking-glass, it's a Revealer. It reveals what's really there, not just what you can see. What it's revealing to you is an underground stream," said Dr. McKracken.

Kitty studied the underground stream again through the Revealer. Blue light twisted like a snake toward the house. She followed it across the lawn and reaching the back door, looked up. Peering through the Revealer she saw the light shimmer all the way down the passageway before disappearing under the door of the forbidden room.

"Oh dear..." she said.

"What is it?"

"The blue rippling light, I mean the underground stream, it flows right down the passageway and under a door."

"Ah..." said Dr. McKracken

"That can't be good," Kitty said, turning to face him.

Dr. McKracken rubbed his hands together and his brow creased. "The story goes that there used to be a well, the old Penny Well I think it was called, right about where your grandparents' house is now, when this land housed a convent. When these houses were built it was covered over."

"Just a well? That doesn't sound too bad."

"The Penny Well was no ordinary well, it was a wishing well."

"Did it work? I mean did it actually grant wishes?" Kitty spluttered excitedly.

"Ask your grandparents, I'm sure they'll tell you all about it."

Kitty glanced away. She had the feeling that her grandparents would not tell her anything. She was certain they were already keeping secrets.

5 THE BAD PENNY

"YOU'RE SURE you'll be alright by yourself?" Grandma asked, opening the front door.

"Of course she will, won't you Kitty?" Grandpa didn't wait for a reply before adding, "We'll be back by lunch time."

The front door closed with a thud. Kitty stood alone in the hallway, suddenly aware of the loud tick-tock of the grandfather clock. She turned and walked into the kitchen and up to the window. Splashes of rain hit the glass panes. The garden looked sodden and glum.

Kitty wondered where her grandparents were going, they said they were going to visit a friend for tea. It sounded boring. But she couldn't help pondering why they hadn't invited her. Sighing, she wandered into the living room.

It was a grand room with polished wooden floors, long red curtains, a piano, and an old bookcase. She ran her finger along the book spines.

The sofa and chairs huddled around a huge fireplace. Next to it was a cupboard door. Kitty opened it, expecting shelves or books, or neatly folded tablecloths. To her surprise, it was dusty and mostly empty, except for a rusty old bucket.

The bucket looked ancient and the rust had eaten a huge hole in the side. It was covered in cobwebs. No one had been in here for a very long time.

Kitty was about to close the door when she noticed a spider disappear into the corner. The cupboard was not very deep, perhaps only deep enough to stand upright in and close the door. She stepped inside. From this angle, she could see that the short wall was not quite straight. She reached out her hand and touched it. The wall swung open with a groan.

A secret doorway.

Could this be the doorway between the houses that her grandparents had told her about? She peered into the darkness. With the light filtering in from the living room, she could make out the beginnings of a very narrow passageway, leading up a flight of stairs. An old candle and matches sat on a narrow shelf just inside the opening. Lighting the candle and holding it aloft, she entered the passageway and began to climb.

A dry, dusty smell filled her nostrils and the wooden steps creaked with every step. The flame flickered. A draft? There must be another door ahead.

The stairs leveled off onto a narrow landing. Walking forward, she reached what appeared to be a dead end. Next to it another set of narrow steps led upwards. Deciding to explore the rest of the passageways later, Kitty held the candle up to the dead end and the flame flickered again. She groped around in the darkness, her free hand searching for a handle. Finding a narrow indentation in the wood, she pushed.

Dust and cobwebs fell down on her head, snuffing out the candle. She spluttered in the darkness, trying to brush them away and open her eyes. Reaching out, she pushed against the wood, it opened a little more and then hit something on the other side. *Stay calm,* she said to herself. After a few seconds, her eyes adjusted to the darkness and she could just make out a sliver of light ahead.

She squeezed herself through the narrow opening and felt something tickly move over her face. As she tried to brush it away, she tripped and fell on her knees, the snuffed candle falling from her hand. Her nose filled with the smell of mothballs and boot polish. Crawling forward she banged her head and fell, tumbling into the light of a second floor bedroom.

Propping herself up on one elbow, she looked back at the cupboard she had just tumbled out of. It was filled with old frilly dresses hemmed with feathers, sequins, and tassels. She had stumbled upon rows of sparkly shoes and hit her head on a large hatbox.

Kitty crawled back into the cupboard to retrieve the candle. She found it lying in among the neat rows of shoes, but to her horror, she realized the hot wax from the candle had splattered the bottoms of the glittering dresses, leaving a trail of pale waxy beads over them all. Kitty sat back wondering how on earth she was going to fix this mess.

"Kitty! We're home!"

Kitty's heart sank.

They haven't been gone long. She looked across the room at a clock and was startled to learn that somehow, over an hour had passed.

Footsteps sounded up the stairs.

Oh no, that'll be Grandma and she'll be coming to this room.

Kitty hurried back into the cupboard. Pushing her way through the ballroom gowns, she half stumbled on the candle and candleholder. She picked them up, pushed the false inside wall open and groped for the shelf where the matches were. There was just enough light filtering in for her to strike a match.

The candle flared to life.

Kitty closed the opening behind her and held the candle aloft. Retracing her steps she reached the secret door to the living room cupboard. Only to hear Grandpa's footsteps enter the living room.

I can't get out that way…

Turning around, the light from the candle revealed another flight of steps going down. They must go to the basement. Kitty followed them to a dead end and a door with a round doorknob.

She twisted and pushed. Nothing happened. She pulled, still nothing. Putting the candle down on the last step, she threw her body weight against the door, falling through and landing in her own room.

Looking back she realized the tapestry hanging by the fireplace concealed this door.

She would have to explore the rest of the secret passageways another time.

"Oh, there you are," Grandma said when Kitty walked sheepishly into the kitchen. Grandpa was already in his chair behind his newspaper. "Tea?" The kettle whistled to a boil while Grandma laid out china cups and saucers.

Kitty noticed that a lot of Grandma's ornaments were dancing bears. Following Kitty's gaze Grandma said, "I used to be a dancer myself you know."

"Oh?" said Kitty.

"I still have all my ballroom dresses and shoes upstairs," she said, filling the teapot. "Would you like to see them?"

Realizing that she had just splattered hot candle wax all over them, Kitty glanced around for a distraction.

Grandpa turned the page of his newspaper.

"Actually, actually..." she stammered and walked over to the window so that Grandma couldn't see her face, which she was sure looked guilty. "I was wondering about...." She looked into the garden and through the drizzle, her eyes settled on the funny old wall at the end of the garden. "I was wondering about the... wall at the end of the garden," she almost shrieked the last few words, grateful to have thought of something to say that did not involve ballroom dresses or sparkly shoes.

"Ah, well now, that wall is ancient."

Grandpa's spectacled eyes peered over the top of his newspaper and glittered before retreating back into the depths of his broadsheet.

"It's much older than the house," Grandma began.

"I was wondering why it looks so higgledy-piggledy," said Kitty. "Like it was smooshed together and then sank."

"It was once the outer boundary wall of the old convent," Grandma continued, "the convent of St. Katherine. It was built in the sixteenth century."

"Katherine? That's my name." Kitty came back to the table and sat down, all thoughts of wax splattered dresses forgotten. "How big was the convent?"

"Around two acres. All of the houses on this street were built in the old convent garden—long after the nuns had left of course."

Grandma sipped her tea thoughtfully before adding, "There was once an entrance into the nuns' garden through that boundary wall in what is now Dr. McKracken's property next door. But I think it was bricked up a long time ago."

"The wall is the only structure of the convent to survive to this day." Grandma poured some tea into Kitty's cup and pushed a plate piled with cupcakes toward her. "Well, except for one..." She paused and then said, "Our village library was built on the foundations of the old chapel."

"How can you build one building on top of another?" asked Kitty.

"Much of Edinburgh is built on the foundations of the older city beneath," said Grandpa, laying the newspaper down on his knee and picking up his teacup. "We'll take you to Edinburgh and you can explore the catacombs under the city if you like."

"Yes please," said Kitty. "Can we go for my birthday?"

"What a good idea," said Grandpa. "In fact, I do believe there is a parade on Midsummer's Eve, perhaps we should all go together?"

"Yes!" Kitty jumped with excitement.

"Well, there you have it," said Grandma. "One last thing, although the chapel was ruined, the foundations were strong, so instead of building from scratch, the library was simply built on top."

"Quite right," said Grandpa. "And I believe they still use the crypt as extra storage for the old books." He chuckled.

"Oh stop it," Grandma scolded. "You'll frighten poor Kitty out of going to the library."

"No, he won't," Kitty said.

"When you go to the library, take a look at the gargoyles guarding the doorway," Grandpa said. "They are quite beautiful. The story goes," he lowered his voice, "that if anyone evil tries to enter the library, the gargoyles scream."

Kitty's eyes widened. "What about the old well?"

"You mean the Penny Well?" asked Grandpa.

Kitty nodded.

"We're told that an underground stream that feeds the well does flow around here somewhere, possibly under this house," Grandpa said.

"We had a strange flood a few years back," said Grandma.

"In the basement," Grandpa said. "What a mess."

"Oh stop it. We don't want Kitty to worry."

"I don't think she's worried." Grandpa's eyes twinkled.

Kitty sipped her tea while she looked out at the garden. Her grandparents did not seem to know any more than Dr. McKracken about the old wishing well.

Two cats sheltered outside under the old plum tree. The larger of the two was orange, the other tan. Kitty wondered if they knew they were sitting on an ancient convent wall and if they did know, would they even care. Kitty squinted. The cats seemed to be staring straight at her.

"Looks like the rain has stopped at last. Might be good for you to get some fresh air," Grandpa said without looking up from his newspaper.

He was right, the rain had stopped, although Kitty couldn't figure out how he knew this. She put down her teacup, grabbed one of the small cakes from a plate on the table and sang, "Bye!" Skipping out of the kitchen door, she headed for the garden.

The door opened with a groan, scraping along the flagstones. The puddle in the middle of the lawn had grown. Kitty glanced at the old convent wall, but the cats who were staring at her a moment before, were gone.

She turned around to go back inside when her shoe scraped against something. Looking down, a big shiny coin caught her eye. It wasn't just shiny, it glowed. Kitty reached out her hand to pick it up.

"I wouldn't do that if I were you."

She spun around so fast she almost fell over. Standing behind her was the big ginger cat. She glanced behind the cat, searching for the source of the voice.

"Ahem!" The cat cleared his throat. He sat upright and waited patiently. "Down here."

Kitty looked at the ginger cat with wide eyes.

"Allow me to introduce myself. My name is Nutmeg," said the ginger cat. "And that shiny thing is a bad penny. Don't touch it."

Kitty's mouth dropped open.

Nutmeg raised his eyebrows. "Did you understand what I just said?"

Kitty nodded, still gawping like a fish.

"You're a strange one…" Nutmeg shook his head.

Regaining the use of her mouth, Kitty spluttered, "I'm strange, I'm strange? You're the talking cat!"

"And you're a witch—otherwise you wouldn't be able to hear me."

Kitty's mouth fell open again.

Nutmeg studied her carefully. "You didn't know that, did you?" He waited for a response. When none came, he shook his head and said, "Oh dear, this is worse than I thought."

A cream and brown cat with beautiful turquoise eyes slunk out from behind a watering can, joining Nutmeg. "Don't you have any powers, any powers at all?" she purred.

"Kitty, allow me to introduce Baby, Baby meet Kitty Tweddle, our witch."

"Sorry, where are my manners, it's a pleasure to meet you, Kitty," said Baby inclining her head in a bowing gesture.

Kitty's mind reeled. Not one, but two talking cats, and if that wasn't enough, they insisted that she, Kitty Tweddle, was a witch. Of all the ridiculous things. She prided herself on her common sense and practical nature. She was not a witch with magic who talked to cats.

Kitty peered from side to side, and then to where the kids next door lived, suddenly suspicious that this was a prank of theirs. She couldn't see them. Both cats looked at her, waiting for her to speak.

"Well," Baby repeated. "Do you have any powers?"

"No."

Nutmeg and Baby exchanged glances.

"You're going to need some," said Nutmeg. "And fast too. There's a rogue wishing well about to erupt around here any minute and we need a powerful witch to stop it. And you're the only witch for miles around."

"You live right here which really does make it your problem," said Baby.

"I'm not a witch. I am sensible and scientific!" Kitty screeched.

Baby crossed in front of Nutmeg. "Exactly what we were hoping for," Baby lied. "Perhaps you might be interested to read more about... things?"

Sensing her intrigue, Baby quickly continued. "There is a book in the library which might be of scientific interest to you."

"What's this book about?" Kitty crossed her arms.

"Magic," Nutmeg said muscling in, bored with the conversation. "Kitty Tweddle, you are a witch and if you don't have the magic needed to close down that wishing well, you need to learn it, fast."

"No, I don't. I don't need to do anything. I'm not reading your stupid magic book and I am going to pick up this penny!"

Nutmeg grimaced and covered his eyes with his paws. Baby darted behind the watering can.

Thick gray clouds rolled overhead and a rumble sounded in the distance. Kitty bent down and picked up the bad penny.

WHOOSH! The wind whipped through her hair.

"There see," she said holding it up. It glimmered.

CRACK!

Thunder rumbled, lightning flashed and rain pitter-pattered down around them.

"Oh no," said Baby emerging from behind the watering can. "Your face!"

Nutmeg peered out from behind his paws and broke into a grin. "Could have been worse."

Kitty turned around, saw her reflection in the window, and screamed.

6 MAGIC POTIONS

KITTY SAT IN the kitchen with big splodges of pink calamine lotion all over her face.

Grandpa peered closely at her while another angry boil bubbled on the end of Kitty's nose.

"They will go away before my birthday, won't they? I don't want to miss the Midsummer's Parade," said Kitty glumly.

"Hmm..." Grandpa looked sideways at Grandma. "Better call for Dr. McKracken."

"Why him?" Kitty asked.

"Well, he was a doctor before he retired, perhaps he can do more for you than this calamine lotion is doing." He nodded toward the half used bottle.

Grandma scurried away to fetch him and a few minutes later, Dr. McKracken entered the kitchen with a concerned look on his face. He put his black leather doctor's bag on the kitchen table. Opening it, he searched around and brought out an instrument. "Say ARRRR."

"Aaarrr."

He looked down her throat and peered inside her ears,

first left, then right and satisfied, turned off the light. "I may have a poultice that could help," he said. "You'll have to come to my office next door."

Kitty sighed, then got up and followed Dr. McKracken to his house. It was a mirror image of her grandparents' house inside. His office was in the attic.

The first thing Kitty noticed when she entered was the smell. Or rather smells, like an orchestra of pong all jostling for her nose's attention. She sniffed musty herbs, citrus flowers and something rather unpleasant that made her nose wrinkle.

Stepping into the wood-paneled room, floorboards creaked underfoot. A glass prism hung in the room's only window, grabbing twinkles of light and throwing them all over the walls. A small wooden desk and chair sat beneath it.

Kitty ducked under bunches of herbs hanging from the ceiling. The walls were covered with shelves laden with bottles of potions, pots of salves, and jars of pickled looking things Kitty could not identify. One wall of the room was a library of sorts with old books stacked from floor to ceiling, their leather spines faded with age. "Do all doctors have this stuff?" Kitty asked, casting her eyes over the jars and bottles.

"Well, in addition to my medical training, I also studied herb lore, alternative medicine and... other remedies." Dr. McKracken pointed up to the racks of drying herbs overhead. "Take rosemary for example, grows in most gardens, tastes wonderful roasted with chicken or potatoes, but did you know it kills bacteria?" He turned and pulled a twig out of a pot on the desk and held it up. "Or a humble stick of licorice can help some people with their blood sugar?" He put the stick in his mouth and chewed while handing one to Kitty. "And chamomile flowers brewed into a tea can help you to fall asleep! Plants are marvelous things, truly marvelous."

"Now, let's take a proper look at you. Sit here please." Dr. McKracken pulled out the chair for Kitty to sit on. He tilted her face from left to right. "Hmm..." He opened a large trunk on the floor that Kitty hadn't even noticed and pulled out an unusual instrument that had the look of a magnifying glass—only with dials and cogs. Using it to examine Kitty's face, his hands adjusted some of the cogs. They clicked and whirred then a different lens snapped into place. He peered through the instrument again.

"Did you touch anything... unusual, before this happened?"

Kitty lowered her head and sighed. "The penny," she whispered.

"What's that now? A penny?" He raised his eyebrows. "What sort of penny?"

"A very old looking one that... well, it glowed."

"Where is it now?"

"I dropped it in the garden when this happened." Kitty pointed to her face.

"I see..." Dr. McKracken leaned back against the wall and waited.

Kitty swallowed and reluctantly told Dr. McKracken the whole story. From how she stumbled across the strange penny, the talking cats, all the way up to the moment boils broke out over her face.

"The cats told you that you're a witch?"

Kitty nodded.

"Hmm..." Dr. McKracken considered her response. "This book of magic they spoke of, do you have it?"

"No, but—you believe that the cats actually talked?"

"Of course cats can talk." He waved a dismissive hand.

"The cats said they could help me to get the book."

"Help often comes in the most unexpected forms. You would be wise to accept the cats' help," said Dr. McKracken.

He stood and scanned his shelves, fingers hovering over each odd shaped bottle. "No, not this one... this won't do! Hmm, perhaps." He took a large round jar down from the shelf, opened its wide stopper and using a spatula, scooped out a little red goo and spread it on one of Kitty's boils. In response, the boil rippled and grew to twice the size. "No! not this one." He quickly replaced the stopper and put it back on the shelf.

Picking up a tall green bottle, he popped the cork. Mist rose from the lip and drifted through the air toward Kitty. Her boils begin to bubble and turn blue. "Definitely not," he muttered and stoppered the bottle, returning to his shelves.

"Not for bewitchments, no, not werewolfery," he said, continuing to search his shelves. Suddenly, he stopped.

"I wonder..."

He picked up a tiny glass vial sealed with black wax. Dark purple liquid squirmed within it like a snake. He spun around to look at Kitty, his eyes narrowed, and then carefully he broke the wax seal. He dipped a small twig into the bottle and lightly touched the boil on the end of Kitty's nose. It quivered, squeaked and shrank.

"That tickles!" Kitty giggled.

"Well, well." He raised his eyebrows.

Dr. McKracken treated all of Kitty's boils, and one by one they disappeared.

"Do you know what's in this bottle?" he asked, watching the purple liquid writhe within its glass cage.

Kitty shook her head.

"You might think that it's a powerful medicine, antibiotic

or some herbal ointment. And you would be wrong. It's none of those things. It's an antidote. Not to poison from a deadly snake nor a scorpion's venom." Turning to face Kitty, he held up the tiny vial and replaced the stopper. "This bottle contains nothing less than the antidote to wishes."

The expression on his face made Kitty shudder. "The antidote to wishes?" Kitty repeated. "I don't understand."

Dr. McKracken gave her an appraising look and then walked back to his shelves. Carefully, he replaced the little vial. "How much do you know about wishing wells?"

"You throw coins in and make a wish."

"And do those wishes come true?" He stood still, facing the shelves of bottles, his back to her.

"No, that would be silly, I mean, they're not real, they can't be real..." Kitty's words trailed off.

Dr. McKracken spun around. "Were those boils on your face real?"

Kitty had to admit, the boils on her face were very real indeed. "But I didn't wish for them."

"No, you didn't, but someone else did. A very long time ago I suspect. You were merely the unintended recipient of a very old, very real, and very powerful wish."

His brow creased with worry, Dr. McKracken returned to his bookshelves. He began pulling out books, one after another, and then carried them over to his desk where he dropped them with a heavy thud.

"Wishing wells are not merely places to throw coins. They are connected to Fairyland." Dr. McKracken glanced at Kitty. "There are cracks in our reality where magic seeps through. Wishing wells often appear at these places, where the magic of Fairyland leaks into our world."

He bent down so that he was eye to eye with her and

whispered, "Wishing wells are filled with magic. It is neither good, nor bad, but responds to the intentions of the wish maker."

Kitty stared.

"Kitty, you must promise me that if you see any more of those old coins lying around, that you will not pick them up. Don't even touch them! Do you understand me?"

Kitty nodded. She didn't want to get any more boils. Or something worse, not that she could imagine anything worse than a face full of itchy boils.

He began to flick through the first book, threw it aside and moved on to the next.

Noticing a piece of paper sticking out from under a small set of brass scales on the desk, she pulled it out and studied it. At the top was her name and date of birth. That she could read. But the rest of the page was covered with strange symbols that Kitty did not understand.

"What's this?" She held it up.

"Patient records." Dr. McKracken pulled the paper from her hands. "It's not the first time you've been my patient."

"Really?" Kitty couldn't remember being Dr McKracken's patient before. In fact, she couldn't remember ever meeting him before arriving at her grandparents' for the summer. She supposed he must be talking about when she was born.

Dr. McKracken opened the top left-hand side draw and shoved the paper inside. "Well," he said, "it seems the boils have gone. Best run along if I were you. And if your cat friends are still around, you might want to take them up on their offer of assistance with obtaining the book of magic."

Kitty got up off the chair and walked to the door. As she opened it to leave the room Dr. McKracken said, "Remember Kitty, things are not always what they seem."

She nodded, turned, and walked through the door and down three flights of stairs, wondering if she would be able to find the cats. She was still thinking these thoughts when she opened the front door and almost tripped over Nutmeg.

"Oye!" he shouted. "Careful!"

"Oh, I'm so sorry!"

"Of all the places in the whole universe a human could put their big feet, it has to be in the place already occupied by a cat," said Nutmeg reproachfully.

"I said I was sorry."

Nutmeg scowled.

"Kitty, you look so much better," Baby's voice soothed. "The boils are all gone."

Kitty clasped her own face, almost to reassure herself. "Yes, and I don't want anything else to happen." She looked at the two cats. "You mentioned a book I should read?"

"Oh, now you want the book?" Nutmeg grumbled.

"Of course." Baby scooted in front of Nutmeg to walk alongside Kitty. "It's in the library. It's not far. It should still be open if we hurry."

"Let me stop by my room on the way. We'll just walk around to the back door, no need to go through the house," Kitty said.

"Hello Kitty," said Marcus Snodgrass, the boy next door, leaning on the fence.

"Oh, um, hello," Kitty replied.

"Who are you talking to?" He looked around her.

"Nobody."

"OK, well, um, terribly sorry about my stupid sister the other day." His brow furrowed. "She's, you know, stupid."

"Um... OK," said Kitty.

"So I was wondering," Marcus continued. "Perhaps we

could get together in the summerhouse, I'll bring some friends along and introduce you."

"What summerhouse?"

"The one in your grandparents' back garden," Marcus said.

"Um..." Kitty stalled, not really knowing what to say. She just knew there was more to this idea than Marcus was willing to share. A wobbly feeling in her tummy told her to say 'no' and get away fast. "I'll have to ask," she said and started to walk away. The cats trotted close to the fence so that Marcus couldn't see them.

His eyes widened in alarm. "No need for that!"

Knew it! thought Kitty. I just knew he was up to no good. He doesn't want my grandparents to know.

"Well, we can talk another time. Nice to see you again Kitty," Marcus called after her.

Waving behind her, Kitty kept walking.

"That was a lucky escape," hissed Nutmeg form under the bushes.

"I know, I just don't trust him," said Kitty.

"Neither do I," said Baby.

Kitty rounded the corner of the house and almost got to the back door. "Oh no!"

"We're too late," both cats said together.

Water ran like a small stream out of the back door and into the garden, making the back lawn more boggy than ever. Grandpa stood in the garden wearing Wellington boots and rubber gloves, shaking his head. "Don't worry Kitty, your room is safe and dry."

Kitty twisted her body to look inside. The water was flowing from under the door of the forbidden room, along the hallway and out the back door.

"Kitty? Kitty dear?" Grandma appeared behind her at the side of the house. "Come inside away from this mess."

Turning around Kitty saw no sign of the cats. Not knowing what else to do she followed her Grandma through the front door. Walking straight into the kitchen, she plopped down on one of the chairs.

Grandma smiled and said, "I'll put the kettle on in just a moment." Then she disappeared, closing the kitchen door and leaving Kitty alone.

The door didn't latch and slowly opened, allowing Kitty to hear voices in the next room. She moved closer to the door to hear more.

"We have to tell her, we really must!"

Kitty recognized Dr. McKracken's voice.

"No! I absolutely forbid it!" Grandma said.

Kitty noted something in her Grandma's voice she had never heard before. Fear.

Footsteps sounded on the stairs coming up from the basement.

Grandpa's voice joined the conversation. "The water, wherever it came from, seems to have stopped."

"You know very well where it came from," said Dr. McKracken. "The wishing well. It's in your basement. You know what this means?"

"We had a little flood years ago—you remember? Nothing happened then, just a bit of water after a long bout of rain, I really think you're over reacting," Grandpa said.

The voices became muffled after that, as if someone had closed the door to the room they were in. Unable to hear anything more, Kitty sighed. So, there really was a well in the basement. Kitty wondered why they wouldn't tell her about it. And why was her Grandma so afraid?

7 THE LIBRARY

KITTY WOKE UP to another gloomy morning. She slipped out of bed, dressed and walked into the hallway. The flagstones felt cool on her bare feet but at least they were dry, scrubbed clean after yesterday's floodwater from the forbidden room. Fortunately, only water had flown from the wishing well and no bad pennies had shown up.

She couldn't wait to tell the cats about the conversation she had overheard between her grandparents and Dr. McKracken. They were keeping something from her all right, and it was all to do with the wishing well.

Turning the key, she pulled the back door open with a tug. Although it wasn't raining, mist rolled across the garden. She stepped outside and looked around for Nutmeg and Baby. Through the fog she could just make out two shapes sitting on the wall under the plum tree.

She took a step forward, tripped and threw her hands out to break her fall. Something cold and round pressed against her left hand.

"Oh no."

Instantly, her head grew hot and itchy.

"What happened to your hair!" shrieked a nasty little voice from next door.

Kitty turned to see the grinning face of Emily Snodgrass.

"You look ridiculous," Emily said, laughing. "Those pink bows." The girl pointed. "What are you thinking?" She disappeared from view, her laughter echoed in Kitty's ears.

Pink bows? What on earth is she talking about? Kitty never wore pink. Never. And bows? She wouldn't be seen dead with pink bows in her hair.

Just then, Nutmeg and Baby trotted out from the mist toward her. Both of them looked at her in wide-eyed alarm.

"What happened to your hair?" asked Nutmeg.

Reaching up with both hands, Kitty felt something massive and bouncy on top of her head. She stood up and tried to pull it off. "Ouch." It was attached to her head. She peered at her reflection in the window.

Kitty screamed.

"Look at me! Just look at me!" she wailed, pulling on long blond curly locks. Peppered with bright pink frilly bows, the big golden ringlets added at least five inches to her height. Emily was right, she looked ridiculous.

"Hsssssss!" Nutmeg winced as a small stone hit him in the side.

"I got your cat! I got your cat!" Emily chanted.

Kitty picked up the stone and threw it back. Being a good aim, she hit Emily right on the forehead. Emily screamed then burst into tears and ran away.

"What's going on? What's all this screaming?" Grandma came running down the stairs into the basement. "Kitty, what happened to your hair?"

"Um…" She remembered what her Grandpa had said the night she arrived, *we don't believe in magic and superstition in this house.* "It's a wig," she lied, not knowing how else to explain having just fallen on a magical bad penny and getting someone else's ancient wish.

"Can you please explain why your nasty little granddaughter has just attacked my precious child?" demanded a snooty voice from next door. Kitty looked up to see Mrs. Snodgrass. Her mouth, outlined in red lipstick, turned down at the corners. Her green eyes gleamed with disapproval.

"Mrs. Snodgrass," Grandma said with a smile. "I've just run outside to find out what's going on myself."

Kitty was quite sure that Grandma wasn't smiling on the inside.

"This girl," Mrs. Snodgrass bellowed, pointing a skinny finger at Kitty, "has just thrown a rock at my daughter's head. Explain yourself child!"

"It wasn't a rock, it was a stone and—"

"So you admit it?"

"Well, I—"

"Did you or did you not throw a stone at my child?"

"But she—"

"Insolent girl!" Mrs. Snodgrass seethed. "Answer the question, did you throw a stone at my Emily, yes or no?"

"Tell the truth dear," Grandma urged.

"Yes."

"Outrageous! I demand she is punished. I demand she be beaten and—"

"I'll take care of any punishments to be administered." Grandma cut her off. "I assure you Mrs. Snodgrass, I'll get to the bottom of this. Kitty, come inside at once."

Grandma ushered her inside and upstairs to the kitchen where Grandpa was reading his newspaper.

"Now Kitty, tell me what happened."

Kitty quickly explained everything.

"Oh dear…" said Grandma.

"Quite right too," said Grandpa from behind his news-paper. "Always stand up for yourself and for small animals who can't defend themselves."

"You're not helping dear," Grandma chided.

"Anyway, forget the stones Kitty, what happened to your hair?" asked Grandpa. He peered over the top of his news-paper, eyebrows knitting together in a frown.

"It's, um, a wig, I was playing dress up."

"It's a little early for that," said Grandma looking at the clock. "Well, best take it off then. I suppose we'll have to think up some punishment to appease Mrs. Snodgrass."

"You're going to punish me? Are you serious?"

"Yes, you can't go throwing stones at people's heads. Even if they are nasty little pieces of work who are cruel to cats. Now run along, there's a good girl."

Kitty sighed and turned to leave the room. She dragged her feet down the stairs into her basement. What a horrible start to the day. She had fallen on a bad penny, gotten bewitched with the ugliest hair in the world, had a fight with the nasty neighbor, the most horrid girl ever, and now she was going to be punished for defending her friend Nutmeg. This day just couldn't get worse. She reached her bedroom and looked into the mirror.

"What am I going to do with this hair?"

"Got a hat?" Nutmeg was lying on her bed, licking his side where the stone had hit him. Baby sat next to him looking concerned.

"It's a bewitchment from the penny you fell on. I'm sure it will wear off soon enough," Baby said.

Kitty tried to remove the bows. Every time she pulled one

out, it reappeared. She tried to brush out the ringlets, but they sprung right back. "This is impossible," she moaned.

"I hate to rush your beauty routine," said Nutmeg, "but we really do need to get along to the library."

Kitty pushed a scarlet headband over her head to hold down the ringlets and struggled to braid the unruly tresses onto something manageable. She finished off by grabbing a red baseball cap. Tugging it down, it hid most of the bows.

"Well, this will have to do," she said, being practical.

The sky was heavy and gray when Kitty and the cats set off for the library. They had just passed the front gate when the rain began to pitter-patter down on them. She pulled up her hood while the cats trotted close to the walls for shelter.

As they walked, Kitty wondered what punishment her grandparents would decide upon for her. Maybe they would make her stay indoors and scrub floorboards with a toothbrush. No, that would be too silly. Perhaps she would have to wash the dishes for the rest of the holidays. No, that would just be too horrible. And, Kitty thought, a little severe considering her crime was defending Nutmeg, something she was quite sure her Grandpa approved of.

She was still mulling over the possibilities when she almost tripped on the front step of the library. She looked up a set of stone steps to see an enormous wooden door. It was at least ten feet high and covered with iron studs.

Walking up the steps, she looked for the gargoyles. She was sure her grandparents had said there were two gargoyles guarding the door. But there were none.

"Hmm... Perhaps the gargoyles are somewhere else," she said.

Nutmeg and Baby looked around nervously, worried about being caught going into the library where cats were not allowed. They were not paying attention to gargoyles or what Kitty had just said about them.

"Make sure no one is watching and we'll come in with you when you open the door," said Nutmeg. "Once we're in, we'll meet up with our inside man."

Cautiously looking around, Kitty pulled open the heavy door. "You have an inside man?" It swung open on well-oiled hinges and they were inside in an instant.

"Yes, well, inside cat, Roger. He's here most days, using stealth and camouflage to avoid detection. He tends to patrol the junior fiction section."

"Patrol? He does not patrol, he sleeps the day away in a comfy chair in the corner," said Baby.

"Same thing," said Nutmeg.

After walking through a small entry hall, they passed another set of double doors into the main reading room. Kitty looked up at the high domed ceiling with intricate gold moldings. Shelves surrounded the round reading room on two levels, with two spiral staircases leading up to the second level of books. Windows encircled the dome above, flooding the room with light.

"The junior fiction section is at the back," hissed Nutmeg.

When they reached the children's section it seemed empty except for a small girl standing alone in front of a saggy-looking black chair.

A shrill scream rang out, breaking the silence.

Kitty froze.

The little girl stared at the old black chair. Two green eyes with slits for pupils stared back at her.

"Be quiet dear," whispered her mother, taking the little girl by the hand and pulling her away. This was a library after all.

"But mummy, the chair has eyes!" wailed the little girl, tears rolling down her cheeks.

Her mother looked back—there was just a black lumpy chair. "There's nothing there dear," her mother huffed.

The little girl looked back and the chair winked at her. "Mummmmmmmmmyyyyy!"

Roger chuckled to himself. How he loved these moments. He would sneak in through the back door and hide in plain sight. An old black cat on an old black chair, quite invisible with his eyes closed.

He settled himself down and went back to sleep to dream catty dreams. Just as well she didn't try to sit on me, he thought, drifting off, she would have found this chair had teeth and claws to go with those eyes... And the lumpy chair twitched while Roger dreamed of terrorizing the library...

Kitty stood with her arms folded across her chest. "That's horrible."

"That's Roger," said Nutmeg.

Baby walked up to him and prodded him with her paw, "Roger! Wake up!"

Roger raised one eyelid. "Well, hello Baby," he said.

"Roger, this is Kitty Tweddle," said Baby, nodding toward Kitty. "The one we told you about. The witch who needs the book of magic."

Roger sat up sleepily. "Kitty," he said and then yawned, flashing his fangs and flexing his whiskers. "Could you do me a favor and help me with my tail?"

Kitty did not move.

"Kitty, I really need your help, my tail has a kink in it, it really hurts, could you help me straighten it? Please?" Roger's eyes looked huge and pitiful. "Just pull it straight… Gently, gently please… Oh, it hurts so much…"

Feeling sorry for him, Kitty reached out for Roger's curled tail and pulled it gently straight.

Roger farted.

"Ugh! That's disgusting!" Kitty couldn't believe she had fallen for the oldest trick in the book.

Roger roared with laughter. He laughed so hard he rolled onto his back and his short legs waved in the air causing his fat tummy to jiggle with each guffaw.

Baby rolled her eyes and mouthed *sorry*, to Kitty.

"Can we get on with this?" said Nutmeg. "Roger, you said you knew where this book of magic was on the shelves. Can you show us?"

Roger's chest still heaved with left over giggles while he half rolled, half tumbled onto the floor. He landed with a thud. "Yes, I can lead you to it." He put his nose to the floor and started following an invisible trail that only he could see.

"What's the book called?" asked Kitty.

"How To Be Witchy, Practical Magic for Everyday Enchantment," mumbled Roger, his nose still glued to the carpet. His nose led him left and then right, then in a circle before he moved forward again, only to stop in the middle of a tall bookcase. "It's up there."

"That's amazing," said Kitty, genuinely impressed. "You can track the book by its smell?"

"No, I knew it was important so I piddled underneath it months ago to mark the spot," said Roger, puffing his chest out with pride.

Kitty rolled her eyes and groaned. "Who is the author?" she asked, scanning the shelves.

"B. Witcher."

After a few moments, Kitty said, "It's not here. The book's not here." There was no reply. She looked around, but the cats had disappeared.

"Can I help you miss?"

Kitty turned around and found herself staring into the face of Mr. Wolf. Now that she was closer to him, she could see he had chocolate brown eyes and dark stubble on his face.

"Kitty Tweddle! My apologies," he said. "I didn't recognize you in the eh... hat..." He coughed. "Allow me to introduce myself properly, my name is Barnaby Wolf and I am the Head Librarian here at the Dribble Library." He held out his hand.

"Oh, yes, how do you do?" Kitty shook his hand. "I remember seeing you on our street in your green car."

"Chartreuse," Mr. Wolf corrected her. "So," he said rubbing his hands together, "anything I can help you find?"

Kitty explained what she was looking for and Mr. Wolf offered to look it up on his computer. Following him to his desk, Kitty glanced around for any sign of the three cats but saw none.

"Hmm... I'm afraid the book has been moved downstairs for repair."

"For repair?"

"I'm afraid it won't be available for many months." He turned away from his computer screen to face her. "What do you want with a book on practical magic anyway?" He raised an eyebrow.

"Oh, just looking for a good read...I'll just take a peek at the junior fiction section." She turned to walk away.

"Have you seen our display book this month? A Field Guide to Ferocious Fairies by Abbey Lubber."

"No." Kitty turned back. She had to admit, she was intrigued. Perhaps it would have some information about the wishing well or at least the bogeyman. "Where is it?"

Mr. Wolf led her to a huge, ancient looking book on a stand. It was open to the contents page. "I'll leave you to it." He smiled before walking away.

Her finger traced down the B's. Noticing three cat heads poke out from behind the nearest bookshelf, Kitty read aloud.

"Banshee, Barguest, Big Ears, Billy Winker, Black Annis, Black Dog, Blue Cap, Bogan, Bogie, Bogie Beast, Bogeyman, Boggle, Brownie, Buttery Spirits." Her brow crinkled. "Hmm…"

Turning to the page entitled Bogeyman, she continued to read.

"Of all the ferocious fairies, the bogeyman, bogie or bogie beast is the most dangerous. Many people believe that stories of the bogeyman exist only to frighten small children who are naughty and will not go to bed. This is not true. The Bogeyman is real and must be avoided at all costs. A changeling, his appearance can take any form, although he will usually revert to a shaggy dog. The bogeyman lives in a bogey hole, which can be a cave, basement, cupboard, bottom of a well or any dark place. It is this author's sincere hope that the reader never meet one of these wicked creatures since such a meeting will most likely end in death."

"What do you think of that?" Kitty turned to face the cats.

"Who are you talking to?" asked a snooty voice behind her.

Kitty turned around to find Mrs. Snodgrass hovering over her.

"As assistant librarian here at the Dribble library, I suggest Miss Tweddle, that you are extremely careful," Mrs. Snodgrass said leaning in. "With the book you are holding." She nodded at the book in Kitty's hands. "I'll be watching."

Kitty gulped.

Mrs. Snodgrass glared.

"I think I ought to be going home now," Kitty said. Stepping back from the book she ducked behind a bookshelf to rejoin the cats.

"There's a back door, let's get out of here," Nutmeg said. He turned and led the way.

They all tumbled out of the library and into the drizzle, hurrying back to Kitty's room.

"She's a right dragon that Snodgrass woman," said Roger, shaking his fur.

"Did you get the book?" asked Baby.

"No, Mr. Wolf said it's downstairs, being mended."

Roger was pacing the floor, all his former bravado gone. "Strange things have been going on in that library. I would know, I've been napping there most days for years."

He sat still and took a deep breath. "It all started when that dragon librarian started working there."

"You mean Mrs. Snodgrass?" asked Kitty.

"That's the one. Anyway, not long after she arrived, some renovations happened. They put down new carpet, moved the furniture around and covered up access to the um... downstairs. Someone has put the book downstairs so that you can't get it, I'd put money on it."

"Well, then, we'll have to go downstairs," said Kitty.

"How will we do that?" asked Nutmeg.

They sat silently and looked at each other.

"What's the problem with going downstairs?" asked Kitty finally.

"Don't you know?" asked Baby.

"No, what's down…" A look of horror spread over Kitty's face. She remembered what her Grandpa had told her about the library being built on top of the old church foundations.

"Downstairs is the old crypt, isn't it?" said Kitty.

Uncertain glances between the cats were all the answer she needed.

8 STARGAZING

"WE HAVE DECIDED on your punishment," said Grandma when Kitty walked into the kitchen for breakfast.

Grandpa turned the page of his newspaper.

Kitty sat down and waited for the worst. Would they force her to apologize to the wretched girl? Wash dishes in their horrible mother's house? Mow their lawns? Be grounded for a week in the basement? Her mind raced over the possibilities, each one worse than the one before. Her shoulders sagged.

"Dr. McKracken next door has had a bit of an accident," Grandpa said while putting his paper down. "He has hurt his wrist and could really do with some help in his garden." He picked up his china teacup and took a sip. "It would be lovely if you would volunteer to help him out."

Kitty couldn't believe her luck. This was it? To help out Dr. McKracken in his garden? "Yes!" she said. "Well, I mean, of course, if that's what you think will be a good punishment."

Grandpa's eyes twinkled.

"I'm sure when Mrs. Snodgrass hears that you have been

punished with helping an elderly neighbor keep his garden up to our neighborhood standards, standards she has rigorously enforced, I've no doubt she will be satisfied."

A big smile spread across Kitty's face. She was so relieved she helped herself to a piece of toast, spreading it with lashings of butter and jam. She had planned on visiting Dr. McKracken anyway to see if he had a potion to cure her ridiculous blond hair. This punishment gave her the perfect opportunity.

"Well, I suppose I could visit him now and get started." She pushed herself away from the table and stood up.

"That's the spirit!" said Grandpa disappearing back into his newspaper.

"Hello!" Kitty called out. Walking into Dr. McKracken's back garden, she found him pottering around, looking at various plants and shaking his head.

"Kitty! Good day to you." He waved a bandaged hand, stood up and took off his cap, patting his bald head with a spotted handkerchief. "Fancy helping me with a bit of gardening?" He squinted when she got closer. "Your hair looks different..."

"I know." Kitty reached self-consciously for her hat and tried to pull it down over the big blond ringlets that had broken free from the braid. She leaned in and whispered, "I accidentally stood on another penny. I don't suppose you have a potion for this?" She pointed at her hair.

"Well, let's go inside and have a cup of tea and a proper look," said Dr. McKracken glancing around. "We need to sort out our gardening plan anyway!" He spoke louder than necessary, just in case someone—like Mrs. Snodgrass—might be listening.

Dr. McKracken's kitchen was the same size and shape as her grandparents', with an old stove and large table. But that's where the similarity ended. Herbs hung on a drying rack overhead while mugs, pans and pots dangled from hooks all over the walls. Kitty had to duck to avoid hitting her head on a huge cauldron suspended by its handle just inside the doorway.

"That one is for making jam." Dr. McKracken nodded toward the big pot.

He worked his way around a stack of books to the stove and put the kettle on. "Now, let's take a look at this hair."

Kitty pulled off the hat and undid what remained of the braid. The blond ringlets sprang out in all directions, like a curly yellow squid.

Dr. McKracken reached for a familiar looking magnifying glass. After squiggling some dials, he inspected the roots of Kitty's hair. "Hmm…" He adjusted the cogs and worked his way around her scalp. "I don't think there is much I can do here but wait for the wish to wear off." He put the magnifying glass back on its hook by the stove. Rummaging around near the sink, he returned with a small mirror and asked, "Has it changed at all since it happened?"

Kitty looked into the mirror. It was still blond and curly, but the color was a little darker and the bows were fewer and less frilly. "I think it's a bit duller." Kitty pulled a ringlet. It had indeed lost some of its bounce.

"We'll see how it looks in a couple of hours," he said. The kettle whistled and Dr. McKracken made them both a cup of tea. He handed a chipped mug to Kitty. "Here, drink this and take your mind off your hair. You never know, after a good day in the garden, it might be almost back to normal."

Kitty raised the mug to her lips and took a sip. It was

sweet and spicy, warming her throat with each swallow. "Wow! This is delicious."

"You can't beat a nice mug of honey and ginger tea," he said.

"Dr. McKracken…" Kitty searched around for the right words.

"What is it?"

"The wishing well, it's in the basement of our house isn't it?"

Dr. McKracken sighed then blinked several times. "About the little flood yesterday, well, your grandparents don't want you to worry you see…" He licked his lips and blinked some more, changing the subject. "So, shall we take these into the garden?" He raised his mug. "There's something I want to show you."

He walked away before she could protest and following Dr. McKracken outside, Kitty felt a raindrop on her face. "I think it's going to rain," she said looking up at a gray sky.

"It is definitely going to rain."

"We're going to get very wet then." Kitty held out her hand, the raindrops were getting heavier.

"Not if we go in here." Dr. McKracken gestured toward the wall at the bottom of his garden.

"In where? There's just a wall."

"Look closely."

Kitty squinted her eyes. It was definitely just a wall. But then she remembered something Grandma had said, about a gateway to the nuns' vegetable garden in the wall on Dr. McKracken's property. Then she saw it. An old archway, its entrance bricked up but unmistakably there.

"Look closer," Dr. McKracken urged. "And remember what I said, things are not always what they seem."

A handle appeared and then a wooden door, where before, there had only been a wall. Kitty pulled the handle downward and the old wooden door swung open with a creak, she moved to duck inside when Dr. McKracken caught her arm.

"Careful!" he warned. "There are precautions we must take." Reaching into his pocket, he pulled out a round silver pocket watch. "This is a Timekeeper," he said. It had a button on top like a stopwatch and it hung on a long silver chain.

"It is not like any ordinary watch. It will keep you in real time and not fairy time."

"What's fairy time?"

"Time passes differently in Fairyland. Many a person has gone into Fairyland for only a few moments, only to return and find that years have passed in the real world," he said nodding gravely.

"To avoid that unfortunate happenstance, press this button before entering the fairy realm." He indicated the silver button. "And press it again when you leave."

Kitty's eyes lit up. She was so excited she thought she would burst.

"Your grandparents forbade me to talk to you about the wishing well, but they were more than willing for you to help me with a little gardening. Although, they didn't specify which garden." He winked and pressed the button on the top of the Timekeeper and they stepped through together.

On the other side, the sun was shining. Bumble bees buzzed lazily around a patch of purple borage, while a tiny fairy sat in the center of a blue flower. Kitty looked closer and noticed that it appeared to be having a conversation with a bumble bee.

"This is the garden I need your help with."

The garden was divided up into quarters, each planted with parsley, sage, rosemary and thyme. Lavender swayed around a sundial in the middle and a red brick wall mottled with vines of yellow, red, pink and purple roses, surrounded it all.

"This is... amazing!" Kitty trailed her fingers through the rosemary releasing its fragrance. She could hardly believe what she was seeing. Bumble bees and fairies flitted everywhere so that the whole place hummed. "It's so alive."

"It is more than alive, it is enchanted. This is a magical garden," said Dr. McKracken.

"Where are we?"

"Fairyland."

"Wow!"

Dr. McKracken's face looked serious. "Kitty, listen very carefully to me, for there are rules that you absolutely must follow here."

Kitty turned to face Dr. McKracken. "What kind of rules?"

"Always remember to push the button on top of the Timekeeper on entering and leaving Fairyland. Oh, and don't trust your eyes, things are not what they seem here." He looked around cautiously, then handed her the Timekeeper.

"It has two other functions." He pressed the bottom of the Timekeeper and the glass lens popped up. "Looking through this lens will show you what is really there. Handy in our real word as well as Fairyland."

"Is this like the Revealer you showed me when I arrived?"

"Exactly!"

Kitty smiled, pleased to have remembered.

"And if you open the back like so." He demonstrated by

pushing the whole back of the device with his thumb. The back of the Timekeeper popped open on invisible hinges to reveal a dark red stone. "Inside lies a Heart Stone. Should you ever get lost, remember—the Heart Stone will always lead back home, no matter how far its bearer wanders."

She studied the Timekeeper carefully, it looked like an ordinary watch. Only she and Dr. McKracken could ever guess that it was so much more. She put the Timekeeper around her neck, the chain was long enough that she could still hold it in her hand. "Now what?" She started to walk toward the sundial in the middle of the herb garden.

Dr. McKracken followed. "Whatever you do, don't touch that—"

Kitty reached out and touched the sundial at that exact moment.

The air around her buzzed like a million bees. There was a flash and a pop, and everything seared white. A moment later, Kitty was plunged into darkness, her eyes still flashing from the sharp brightness. She stumbled back and almost tripped over an old lady.

"Welcome Kitty Tweddle," said the old hag. She was almost bald and sat hunched at a spinning wheel. Wool flowed in a steady stream though her gnarled fingers.

The hag stopped spinning. "You're early."

"Early for what?"

"For your bindings to break. You have the power to enter Fairyland and see fairies. A very powerful witch bound this power at the time of your birth. The binding was to stay in effect until your twelfth birthday."

"That's not for a couple of weeks," said Kitty. "On Midsummer's Eve."

"So like I said, you're early."

The hag pulled her red tartan shawl about her stooped shoulders. Her bottom lip stuck out much further than it should have and she noticed Kitty staring at her disfigured mouth. "This, my dear, is from an eternity of spinning."

Kitty's head was buzzing, a powerful witch bound her powers? What powers did she have anyway? Kitty had not thought of herself as anything but an ordinary girl before coming to her grandparents' house.

"You have many questions, I can see that," said the hag, reading her mind. She went back to spinning as if she had forgotten Kitty was standing there.

"Excuse me, but, why am I here?" Kitty asked.

The old hag continued to spin for a moment and then glanced up at Kitty. "You are here to learn your destiny."

"Which is?"

"Your bindings are unraveling early. This can mean only two things. Either you are extraordinarily powerful. Or, something very bad is about to happen and your powers are needed to stop it. Or both."

"What do you think?" Kitty asked.

"Both," said the old hag without hesitation. "And that hair isn't yours."

Kitty reached up and touched it. "Oh, I know, I was hoping it would go away. I stood on a bad penny from a wishing well."

"Do you believe in coincidences Kitty Tweddle? Do you believe that some things just happen without any reason?" The old hag stood up and took a step toward her.

Kitty wasn't sure. "It's not something I've ever really thought about."

"Well my girl, there are no coincidences. Do you think it's a coincidence that you return to the very house you were born in for your twelfth birthday?" She leaned on a staff and shuffled closer. "Do you think it's a coincidence that your powers were bound until your twelfth birthday? Do you think it's a coincidence that a magical wishing well springs up in the basement of the very house you are living in? Well? DO YOU!" The old hag shook her staff inches from Kitty's face.

"I was born in my grandparents' house? I thought I was born in a hospital, like everyone else..."

The hag studied Kitty's face closely. "You've a lot to learn girl, a lot to learn..."

Kitty blinked. "I do?"

"We all hoped you could stop the wishing well from opening again, but it's too late for that, it's opened, and them that were trapped in it are now free and up to all sorts of mischief. You know who I mean?"

"Um... not really."

"Him! Didn't you see him? The night of the thunderstorm?"

Remembering the dark shape she'd seen at the window during the storm, Kitty shivered. "Yes, I saw."

"Old dog breath... He's back..." The hag sat back down at her spinning wheel and picked up her yarn.

"Dog breath?"

The hag smiled and started spinning again. "The bogeyman must be stopped. You must stop him and close down the wishing well. This is your destiny."

"How?"

"There are two doors in this fairy garden, one to the left and one to the right. Here they are." She gestured to either side. "One leads to the past, the other leads to the future. What question do you most need answering?"

Kitty thought about it for a moment. What she most

needed to know was how to get the book of magic from the library. "Can I find the location of a book and how to get it by using the future room?"

"Yes, you can find out how to do almost anything. But be warned—you will only be shown where the book is and how to get it. You will not be shown what happens after that. Listen very carefully Kitty. All actions have consequences. Many a person has gone ahead and done some noble deed, but then deeply regretted it when the true cost was revealed to them later. Are you prepared to pay the price of getting this book, of reading it and using what you learn? Are you prepared to accept the consequences, whatever they may be?"

"Yes."

The old hag looked Kitty up and down, got up from her spinning wheel, grasped her staff and shuffled toward the door leading to the future. "Follow me," she said without looking back.

The door opened into a small dome shaped room that housed a huge brass telescope. It pointed out through a window at a starry sky, while the rest of the room's walls were covered in charts bearing ancient symbols. Kitty recognized them at once, they were the same symbols she had seen on Dr. McKracken's patient records.

"What do these mean?" asked Kitty pointing to a chart.

"These are star charts. They show the movements of the stars in the heavens and what that means for those of us here on Earth. This is how we can see possible futures."

"What do you mean, possible futures?"

"There are more possible futures than you could ever count or imagine," said the hag. "The future is not certain. Every action is like throwing a pebble into a pond. You may see the stone hit the water but how far with the ripples spread? What will they encounter? We can never know the true extent of our actions on the future. Remember what I said about consequences?"

Kitty held the Timekeeper tightly in her hand. "What is this?" She pointed to the telescope.

"That is a Seeingscope. It responds to questions about the future."

"How does it work?"

"That's simple, just think of your question, think it very clearly in your mind, walk up to the Seeingscope and speak your question out loud. Then, look through the glass and then..."

"Yes?"

"Then..." The old hag raised her eyebrows and in a hushed voice said, "The answer will be revealed to you."

Kitty closed her eyes and concentrated, forming a very clear question in her mind. After a few moments, she opened her eyes and walked up to the Seeingscope. Holding the eyepiece in her hand she said out loud, "Where is the book of magic and how do I get it?" Then she looked into the glass.

Cogs and wheels on the Seeingscope turned as steam belched out from beneath it, enveloping Kitty. The candles flickered and a breeze tickled the star charts, making their edges flutter. The steam cleared while blue and yellow lights glimmered and swirled around her like a starry blanket, wrapping her in magic. The answer popped into Kitty's head like it had been there all along.

"Ah! I know how to get it." Kitty was still looking through the Seeingscope. "I know how to get the book." She turned to look at the old hag. "This isn't going to be hard at all. This is going to be easy!"

The old hag raised an eyebrow but said nothing.

"I know exactly where it is, it's all very straightforward," said Kitty confidently.

"You'll be leaving now I expect?" said the hag. "Just go back out the way you came—and remember to push the button on your Timekeeper the moment you return. It works a bit like a stopwatch. Sort of..."

But Kitty wasn't listening because she was already out of the room and halfway toward the door leading to Dr. McKracken's garden.

The old hag hobbled back to her spinning wheel.

"Thanks for all your help!" Kitty called behind her. "Oh, and so nice to meet you," she said, remembering her manners. She opened the door and stepped through.

"Just remember," said the old hag as she began to spin the wool once more, "there will be consequences... There are always consequences."

But the spinning wheel was the only sound in the room because Kitty had already gone.

9 THE CRYPT

KITTY LEANED against the open back door and stared out at the garden. "All we need is the key," she said.

"What key? And what are you looking so smug about?" Nutmeg scowled. He sat across from her and followed her gaze across the garden to the Snodgrass household.

"You found out something in Fairyland, didn't you?" Baby pawed Kitty's knee.

"Yes, I did." Kitty grinned. "I found a way to get us into the library."

Baby and Nutmeg exchanged worried glances.

"Like I said, all we need is the key, and we all know who has one don't we?"

All eyes turned to the Snodgrass's house.

"Oh, I see where you're going with this." Nutmeg nodded. "Mrs. Snodgrass works at the library so of course she will have a key."

"But Kitty, how are we going to get the key?" Baby asked. "You're not exactly in the Snodgrass's good books. They're not going to just give it to you."

"One of them will. I have something Marcus Snodgrass

wants—access to the summerhouse at the bottom of our garden. He asked me if he could use it not long after I first arrived. He wants to invite his friends over or something."

"But the summerhouse belongs to your grandparents," said Baby. "Won't they mind?"

Kitty waved her question away. "I am going to propose a trade. He will get the library key for me and I will get the summerhouse key for him. We will exchange in the evening and swap back again before sunrise." She crossed her arms triumphantly over her chest. "We'll slip into the library after dark, grab the book, slip out again and lock the door behind us. No one will ever know."

Nutmeg raised his eyebrows, Baby looked at the ground.

"It'll work! I saw it through the Seeingscope in the future room."

"What exactly did you see?" asked Baby.

"I saw a long silver key in Grandpa's key box upstairs, then Marcus and his friends in the summerhouse, then I saw us four in the library at night, and then I saw myself holding the book of magic. That means it has to work."

"I've heard that whatever you see through that Seeingscope always comes with consequences," said Nutmeg. But his voice was drowned out by Kitty's Grandma shouting, "Kitty, dinner is ready!"

"Coming!" Kitty called back.

"Meet me here after dinner," Kitty said to the cats. "We go to the library tonight!"

Kitty's eyes lit up when Grandma opened the oven and pulled out a raspberry sponge pudding. It filled the kitchen with the smell of stewed berries. Even though Kitty had just eaten a plate of roast chicken with all the trimmings, and had seconds, her belly still growled when Grandma served her portion, topping it with a huge dollop of vanilla ice cream. It was delicious and Kitty scoffed the lot, scraping her bowl with her spoon to make sure she got every last taste of it.

Grandpa got up to wash the dishes and Grandma put the kettle on the stove to boil. "We'll have tea in the sitting room?" It was more of a statement than a question.

Kitty smiled. "Sounds great." Pushing herself away from the table, she walked into the sitting room, slumping down on the squidgy sofa in front of the fireplace. Her eyes wandered to the door next to it. A doorway she knew led to a secret passageway.

"Here we are!" Grandma laid a tray down on the coffee table. She poured a cup of steaming tea and handed it to Kitty. Grandpa joined them shortly afterward.

Kitty looked at the clock on the mantle, it was almost 7pm. She would have to be quick. She drank her tea too fast, burning the inside of her mouth. She was almost finished when Grandpa lifted the teapot to pour his cup.

Yawning Kitty said, "All that roast chicken and raspberry pudding is making me sleepy." She stretched. "I think I might have an early night." She stood up trying not to look at the clock again. "I might read for a while first."

Grandpa glanced at the clock. "Rather early for you..." he let his words hang in the air.

"That's fine dear," Grandma soothed.

When Kitty left the room and entered the hallway she heard the grandfather clock click the way it did a few seconds before it chimed. She knew the sound of the chimes would cover the sound of her rattling through the wooden key box next to the clock. She also knew she would only have seven chimes to retrieve the key to the summerhouse. She took another step toward it.

Bong! Bong! Bong!

She raced across the hallway and reached the key box, looking over her shoulder to make sure no one was watching and then flipped open the latch—

Bong!

She searched through the keys, sure it was hanging on the second row in the middle—

Bong!

That's what she had seen when she had peered through the Seeingscope in the star room. Where is it? Why isn't it here? she thought frantically, searching for a long thin silver key.

Bong!

And then she saw it, hidden beneath a larger key on the same hook. She grabbed it, the rattling of metal covered by a final—

Bong!

She silently closed the latch and slipped down the stairs to her basement room and pulled open the window. "I've got it!" She held up the silver key and leaned out to face the three cats. Dangling from the end of the key was a keyring with the word 'summerhouse' written on it in blue ink.

"I'm impressed," said Roger. "Didn't think you had it in you." He turned around, thrust his hind paw into the air, and started to lick his fur.

"Bathing? Now?" asked Nutmeg.

"Well, we can't go until it gets dark and that won't be for hours," said Baby.

"Very well, what's the plan?" Nutmeg shook his head.

All three cats looked at Kitty.

"The plan is—" Kitty stopped mid-sentence.

"Marcus!" She waved, seeing him in the garden next door.

Marcus scowled until Kitty held up the silver key to the summerhouse.

"What's that?" He walked to the fence between the two gardens.

"Something you want. The key to the summerhouse."

His frown quickly turned into a smirk and he beckoned her over.

"But I want something from you in return." She grinned.

It was dark when Kitty crept out of her bedroom and through the back door of the house. She slung a small backpack over her shoulder. Thinking ahead, she reasoned it would be good to have a bag for the book. Walking along the basement hallway to the dresser at the foot of the stairs, she picked up a mini LED lantern by the handle. Some light might be helpful, she thought.

It had been easy getting the library key from Marcus. He was only too happy to exchange it for the summerhouse key so that he could hang out with his friends.

The moon was almost full and cast a shadow that followed Kitty to the wall at the bottom of the garden. She didn't want to risk being seen going through the front gate, which creaked anyway. She crept past the summerhouse to avoid being seen by Marcus and his friends who were already inside and made her way to the old plum tree and waited. One by one, the cats appeared on the wall behind her.

"This way," said Nutmeg and disappeared into the darkness.

Kitty used the tree to scramble onto the wall. She stopped to glance back and make sure she had not been seen. But there were no lights on in her grandparents' house, or either of the neighbors and all of the curtains were closed.

As she turned away, the door to the summerhouse opened and someone stepped out.

She dropped down the other side of the wall.

"No one saw me leave," she whispered to the cats.

They hurried through the dark streets and made it to the back door of the library without any problems.

Kitty pulled the borrowed key from her pocket and inserted it into the lock. "Here goes nothing." She turned it and heard the lock click. All three cats hurried inside first, Kitty followed and closed the door quietly.

Moonlight shone through the windows leaving slashes of light on the carpet, enough for Kitty to see her way to the middle of the bookshelves without the use of her lantern. The cats could see easily in the dark and quickly made their way to the furthest corner of the room.

Once she was in complete darkness and far from the windows, she pulled the lantern out of her backpack and turned it on. It reflected in the cats' eyes, making them look creepy. Kitty took a deep breath.

"Everything OK?" asked Baby.

Roger trotted ahead. "Come on, the entrance is here."

Kitty stood still for a moment, taking in the darkened library.

"What are you waiting for?" snapped Nutmeg.

Kitty followed the three sets of cats' eyes to the corner of the room. "I don't see anything," she said, the light from her lantern searching around the room like a fuzzy spotlight.

"Watch where you point that thing!" said Nutmeg.

"It's right here." Roger pawed at the very corner of the carpet. "You'll have to move the table and chairs out of the way. The entrance to the crypt is a secret doorway set into the wood-paneling on the wall."

Kitty did as Roger said, pulling the small table and chairs out of the way. She stood in front of what looked like a solid wall.

"I don't see a doorway," Kitty said, smoothing her hand over the wood surface, searching for a catch or hidden lever.

She pulled at the edges of the panel. It didn't budge. She heaved again. Still no movement.

"It's stuck!"

Kitty's heart sank. Putting the lantern down on the table she had just moved, she stood with her hands on her hips. She couldn't believe they had gotten this far only to find a locked secret door.

"Try pushing," said Baby.

Working her hands around the edges of the wood-panel, she pushed gently all the way around. "Still nothing." She stood back and cocked her head to one side. "I wonder..."

She pushed the panel right in the middle and it swung open, swiveling on a center post.

Kitty gasped.

All four of them stared into the darkness beyond.

A whiff of something musty escaped on the chilled air rising from the crypt.

"Come on then," said Roger. He pushed ahead past Kitty's calves and disappeared into the dark passageway.

The hairs on the back of Kitty's neck prickled. She picked up the lantern and holding it aloft, walked through the door.

The passageway turned sharply and went down a narrow set of stone steps. Kitty's footsteps crunched on something underfoot. The smell got stronger. Damp, cold and something else that was quite unpleasant.

Reaching the bottom, the stairs turned again and emptied out into a small narrow chamber. It looked like it had been partly carved from the bedrock. Some old shelves stood leaning against the wall nearest to her, books haphazardly piled on top of each other. Further along, Kitty saw what looked like stone coffins. One of the lids was ajar.

Kitty shivered.

A dripping sound echoed around the small chamber and Kitty held the lantern up to see where it was coming from. In the furthest corner from her, a green slime clung to the wall, dripping its way to the floor. "Ugh! This is horrible," Kitty said as she moved the light back along the wall. "I don't see any signs of books being repaired down here."

Then something caught her eye. It looked like a horizontal niche or shelf cut into the rock wall. Kitty walked closer to it, curious to see what it was. She shone the light inside then jumped back, stifling a scream.

Her breath rasped in her throat and she stumbled back against the wall, almost falling into the stairwell. *Pull yourself together Kitty!* She regained her balance and shone the light back onto the shelf, and straight into the dead eye sockets of a human skull.

"Hssssss!"

The sound came from all three cats. Each stood with their backs arched, fangs bared and ready to spring. Their eyes fixed on the back wall of the crypt, where it was darkest.

Kitty's heart pounded, she turned away from the shelf and cast the light toward the cats, trying to see what had spooked them. She couldn't see anything. Calm down! she said to herself. It's probably nothing. After all, we're just all alone in a crypt full of open coffins...

"Find that book fast!" hissed Roger.

"What is it? What are you staring at?" asked Kitty.

Baby turned around to face Kitty. "I'll help you look."

Nutmeg didn't move. He crouched in front of the others, ready to fight anything that came out of the darkness.

Trotting over to the tumble of books, Baby raised herself up on her hind paws to read the titles on the spines. "How To Be Witchy, isn't it?"

"Yes," said Kitty, following Baby over to the ramshackle bookshelves. "How To Be Witchy: Practical Magic for Everyday Enchantment by B. Witcher." Kitty held the handle of the lantern between her teeth and they searched the books together, Kitty starting from the top of the shelves and Baby working upward from the bottom.

Kitty picked up one weighty book with a spine so blackened she couldn't read it. She opened it and a huge black spider sprang out and skittered over her hand and back into the book stacks. Kitty gasped and dropped the book on the flagstone floor. It landed with a thud.

"Leave it and move on," urged Baby without even looking up. The other two cats stood guard in silence.

The books were not stacked in any kind of order that Kitty could see. This made reading the spines difficult and Kitty had to twist her head this way and that.

She scanned through books on gardening, cooking, needlepoint and knitting. She moved to the next shelf and onto car repair, woodwork for beginners and a book on fixing your own toilet.

On the next shelf, she found a small book with a lonely woman on the front cover. She opened it to find mildew growing across its pages. A quick read of the first few sentences and she knew this was a romance novel and not a book on magic.

Kitty and Baby met in the middle of the shelves. "It's not here," said Kitty.

Baby stood back. "What's that over there?" She pointed with her nose. In the wall beside the bookshelves was another shelf carved out of the rock. A few books had slid off the bookshelves and into the niche.

Kitty sighed, knowing that there was probably another skeleton in there.

I can do this, she said to herself. She walked toward the niche, stepping over the big thick book she had dropped and shone her lantern into the dark space. Sure enough, there was a skeleton inside, its jaws wide open in an endless scream.

Ignoring it, she focused her attention on the books. Three were visible. She moved the light over them and whispered the titles, "Herbs for Magic Brews, A Witch's Diary, Astrology for Pets... That's it... It's not here."

"It has to be!" hissed Baby. "Look properly."

Kitty got so close that her head was only inches from the skull. She shone her light down the length of the niche and saw every bone. She stopped about half way down. One book had fallen deeper in and was somehow underneath a skeletal hand.

She knew she was going to have to touch the skeleton to get at the book. Pausing for a moment, she closed her eyes in dread.

"What's wrong?" asked Baby. "Do you see it?"

"Yes, the skeleton is holding a book in its hand, but I can't see which book it is."

"Well, take it out!"

Kitty took a deep breath and reached inside the niche. Prizing the skeletal hand away, she pulled the book free and shone the light on the cover. "I've got it!"

The skeletal hand moved and the fingers fell off, scattering on the floor one by one.

"Let's get out of here, now!" Baby hissed on her way up the stairs.

Roger barged past almost knocking Kitty over.

She staggered backward into a ramshackle bookcase. It wobbled from side to side, and although Kitty reached out a hand to steady it, one by one, the books on the top shelf slid onto the floor.

A low growl made her glance around to see Nutmeg back slowly away form the rear of the crypt, still crouched with his fangs bared.

She lost her grip on the bookcase and more books slid off the top shelves. "I can't hold it!" she cried and the bookshelf groaned, toppling to the floor with a loud crash, spilling books everywhere.

A moment later, a bone-chilling cry rang out in the silence.

"You've woken them up! Get out of here now!" bellowed Roger up ahead, no longer trying to be quiet.

Kitty raced up the stairs after Roger and Baby. Once at the top, she turned around to see Nutmeg come flying through the doorway after her like a ginger bullet.

She quickly closed the secret door and pulled the small table and chairs back into place.

"Hurry!" urged Roger.

Opening her backpack, she stuffed the book and the lantern inside and ran toward the main door. Her shadow followed the cats' shadows, streaking through the silvery moonlight shining through the windows.

Once through the main door, Kitty locked it behind them and they ran together to the street.

They barely reached it when she heard the sound of glass shattering behind them, followed by a horrible scream. She looked back to see one of the library windows smashed and small dark shapes pouring through the hole. Slivers of broken glass lay on the ground, glinting in the moonlight.

"Come on Kitty! Run!" Nutmeg pawed at the back of her knees, his claws sharp against her calves.

One of the creatures from the crypt glared right at her, pointed and screamed again.

Kitty turned and ran out of the library car park and down the street in the direction of home. Risking a glance back, she saw a hoard of the little creatures running down the road after her, jostling each other and squealing, clawed hands outstretched.

What were they? What had she done? Kitty's mind raced.

"Don't look back!" Nutmeg urged from up ahead.

A loud crash sounded behind her. A garbage can rolled past. Kitty screamed when a dark hairy hand grasped for her ankle. She looked down to see the grinning, troll-like face of one of the creatures.

The little hairy thing giggled raucously like it was having the most fun ever.

Kitty ran and didn't stop running until reached the wall at the bottom of the garden.

Gasping for breath, she threw her backpack across it and scrambled over, dropping down among her grandmother's flower beds. The cats were already ahead of her.

Another blood-curdling scream. Further away this time, further down the street. She froze underneath the plum tree. A light went on in a nearby house. Three sets of cats' eyes glimmered by the back door, urging her on.

Grabbing her backpack, she dashed across the lawn.

Twisting the handle and pulling it open, Kitty and the cats tumbled inside and slid straight into her room, stashing the backpack under her bed where the three cats were already hiding. Quickly changing into her pajamas, she jumped into bed.

In the silence, Kitty could hear her heart pounding, sure that any second her grandparents would burst in through the door. But maybe they hadn't heard the awful screams. Perhaps they were deeply asleep. She hoped so.

Finally she asked, "What were those creatures?"

At first none of the cats spoke. Slowly, Nutmeg slunk out from under the bed so that Kitty could see him in a chink of moonlight filtering through the window. He jumped up onto the bed. Kitty propped herself up on one arm.

"Night stealers. Troublesome creatures that sneak into old burial chambers or crypts and nest there. They sleep for the most part. But if they are disturbed, they wake up very hungry —and mischievous—and we've just woken them up."

"That's bad then?"

"I'm afraid it's very bad," said Nutmeg. "And it will only get worse. They cause utter mayhem."

Kitty closed her eyes and her heart sank. How come the Seeingscope had not shown her any of this? Then she remembered what the old hag had said, it only answers your question and nothing more. Kitty had asked the Seeingscope where the book was and how to get it.

Something else nagged at her, something else the old hag had said, something about consequences. The only consequence imaginable was getting caught, not releasing some nasty creatures called night stealers that Kitty didn't even know existed until now.

"Well, we have the book at least," Baby's hopeful voice drifted from under the bed. "Maybe there will be something in there to help us."

"Yes, we've got the book," Kitty replied.

Snoring from under the bed told them that Roger was already asleep.

"I think he has the right idea," said Nutmeg. "Let's all sleep on it and see how things are in the morning."

Kitty tried to sleep but lay awake forever, staring into the darkness, a million questions swirling around inside her head. When she did fall asleep, she dreamed she was locked in a spooky house and every door she opened led her into a cupboard filled with rusty old buckets covered in spider webs.

Like most dreams, she only remembered snatches of it in the morning.

10 BOOK OF SPELLS

KITTY'S STOMACH was in knots when she entered the kitchen the next morning. She wondered if her grandparents had heard the terrible screams from the night stealers escaping the library.

She had already exchanged keys with Marcus Snodgrass. Marcus had kept his word, leaving the summerhouse key on the fence between their houses, just like they had agreed. Pocketing it, Kitty replaced it with the library key.

With the radio playing, Kitty took a seat at the kitchen table. Grandma's back was turned as she busied herself with the stove. Grandpa sat behind his newspaper.

The song playing on the old radio cut to a voice. "We interrupt our usual program for a brief news report. Just in, we are sad to announce news of a mysterious break-in at the Dribble village library last night."

Grandma turned around and twiddled a knob to turn up the volume.

"A window was broken on the ground floor facing the car park, however, nothing appears to have been taken. Police are making enquiries in the neighborhood. Anyone with information leading to the apprehension of the culprits is asked to come forward immediately."

Kitty swallowed hard.

She turned and looked at Grandpa and noticed a picture on the front page of his newspaper with the title—*More Gargoyles Missing!* She strained to read the smaller print when the same news storey was broadcast on the radio.

"And our next news story, another of the City of Edinburgh's gargoyles has disappeared, this time from a church on the Royal Mile. Bafflingly, there is no evidence of its removal, no signs of damage to the stonework or masonry of the buildings. One resident said, 'It's as if the gargoyle just got up and left.' Were it not for old photographs of the gargoyles in place, many would doubt that they had ever been there at all. And now for the weather..."

Grandma turned the volume back down. "Well, what do you make of it Kitty? A break-in at our library and more missing gargoyles."

Kitty looked down at the table, not sure what to say. "Something weird," she mumbled. "Is there any toast?"

Feeling sick after forcing down her breakfast, Kitty went back to her room. Whether she would be found out for the library break-in or not, it was all pointless if she didn't manage to use the book and close down the wishing well. And now that these horrible creatures, night stealers, were on the loose, being able to use some good powerful magic was more important than ever.

She retrieved the backpack from under her bed and took out the book.

Flopping down on the bed, she looked at it. The salmon pink cover was stained with something Kitty decided not to think about. Big gold embossed letters proclaimed this was

How To Be Witchy: Practical Magic for Everyday Enchantment by B. Witcher.

Kitty opened the book and wrinkled her nose. It smelled like the crypt, musty and damp. She flipped through the table of contents, introduction, a very long chapter on protection magic, and then chapters on charms, herbs, teas, tinctures, lotions, potions, oils and vinegars.

There was no mention of wishing wells, night stealers, missing gargoyles or any of the other things on her mind. She sighed, deciding she had better just start reading. She turned to chapter one.

Baby slunk in through the open window. Sensing her presence rather than hearing her, Kitty looked up. "No Roger?" she asked.

"He's at the library, staking things out," said Nutmeg, poking his head through the window. He wriggled through the narrow gap and jumped down onto the bed.

"You mean sleeping!"

"Have you started reading the book?" Nutmeg asked, ignoring her comment about Roger.

"Just starting."

"What does it say?" asked Baby, jumping down onto the bed to curl up next to Nutmeg.

Kitty read aloud. "Place a bowl of salty water under the bed, right around where one's head would be for protection against nightmares. Sprinkle salt in a circle around the bed, also good for protection from slugs. Sugar will do in a pinch. The following herbs and plants are good for protection, garlic, rosemary, sage, and oregano. Contrary to popular belief, garlic will not offer protection against vampires who are rather partial to it." Kitty stopped reading and looked at the cats.

"Vampires love garlic?"

Both cats shrugged.

"I thought they were afraid of it."

"Naaa," said Nutmeg. "It's the vampires who started that rumor. Bet they have a good laugh at it now." He chuckled.

Kitty wasn't laughing. "You've seen vampires?"

"Not recently." Nutmeg looked at his paws. "What else does the book say?" He changed the subject.

"Nothing about wishing wells."

"Well, pouring some salt around your bed couldn't hurt, could it?" asked Baby.

"I suppose not," said Kitty. She got up and went into the kitchen. Rummaging around in the cupboards, she came back with a box of salt and used it to make a wobbly ring around her bed.

"There. It doesn't have to be perfect, right?" She glanced at the cats.

"It's fine," they both said together.

Kitty picked the book up again and continued to read. She flipped through pages on the many uses of rosemary, from adding it to home made soap, to vegetable soup, to stewing it into an antibacterial tea which could also be used to clean floors and dye gray hair brown. "None of this is any use!" cried Kitty. "It's all so very... practical."

"Are you sure you're not missing something?" asked Nutmeg.

"Ah!" Kitty pulled out the Timekeeper and flipped up the lens on the front. "Dr. McKracken said the Timekeeper could also work like a Revealer and show what's really there."

She held the glass of the Timekeeper up against the book and peered through it.

"I can't believe this—it looks just the same!" Kitty wailed, flopping backward onto the bed. She tossed the musty book onto the floor. "I broke into the library, snapped the fingers off an old skeleton, stole a book and released those horrible night stealers for nothing. And who knows when the police will come knocking on the door...I've made such a mess of everything..."

"No, you haven't," Baby soothed. "Don't think that way."

"Maybe there is someone else who could help you understand the book," said Nutmeg.

"Dr. McKracken. He has loads of books about herbs and potions, maybe he can see something I'm missing. I'll go and see him now." Kitty jumped up, grabbed the book and dashed off, leaving the two cats sitting on her bed.

"Dr. McKracken!" Kitty ran into his back garden with the book tucked under her arm. She looked around and saw him next to the wall, bent over a plant. He appeared to be talking to it. Kitty stopped, not wanting to interrupt his conversation, but at the same time eager to get some answers.

Dr. McKracken glanced up. "Kitty! How wonderful to see you."

"Dr. McKracken, I need your help." She thrust the book out in front of her. "With this."

"Is this the book our friend Nutmeg recommended?" he asked.

"Yes," said Kitty, hoping he wouldn't ask how she got it.

"Best take a look then." He wandered off toward a small gazebo at the bottom of his garden. Inside the gazebo were two small chairs and a round wooden table. He laid the book down on the table but did not open it. His eyes crinkled at the corners and he smiled. "Why don't you tell me what's on your mind."

Kitty chose her next words carefully. She explained that Nutmeg said this book contained magic that would help her close down the wishing well and that they had gone to the library together to get it.

She paused there and decided not to mention Mr. Wolf, the librarian, who told her the book was being repaired. She also chose to miss out the part about borrowing a key from Marcus Snodgrass to the back door of the library and sneaking into the crypt to get the book. She definitely missed out the bit about releasing the screaming night stealers.

Kitty continued, "But the book doesn't contain anything about wishing wells that I can see." She glanced at the book and when Dr. McKracken didn't speak she added, "I thought you might know something... some special way of looking at the book or reading it, something I'm not seeing..."

Dr. McKracken took the book and flipped through. "You have looked through the Revealer lens on the Timekeeper I assume?"

"Yes, it looks the same."

"No, I don't see anything on wishing wells either. Maybe like Nutmeg said, you're not seeing it right." His eyes wandered toward the door to Fairyland.

Kitty pulled the Timekeeper out from her shirt and held it up. It caught the sunlight streaming through the trees, making it glitter like a golden jewel.

"I think you could be right," she said, and picking up the book, walked toward the doorway.

"Oye! Running off without us?" said Nutmeg.

"If you're going into Fairyland, we're coming with you," said Baby.

"Ok then, come on." Kitty turned around and faced the wall where the doorway to the fairy garden should be. At first she couldn't see it and felt a twinge of panic. Closing her eyes, she took a few deep breaths. When she opened them, the doorway appeared in front of her.

"Remember to press the button on the top of the Timekeeper!" Dr. McKracken called after her.

Holding the Timekeeper in her hands, she pressed the button and with a cat on either side of her, stepped through the doorway.

They stood together in the fairy garden. Lavender swayed around the sundial in front of them, its scent filling the air. A small creature peeped out from behind it with a grubby face and long floppy ears.

Kitty gazed at the book in her hands. She walked toward the sundial and the small creature disappeared behind a bush. Sitting down on the pathway in front of the lavender, she laid the book down and opened it. To her dismay, it looked exactly the same.

An enormous bumblebee buzzed by, moving from flower to flower. Kitty peered around to see legions of them. She studied the one hovering close to her nose and realized that they were not bumble bees at all, but squat little fairies wearing black and yellow striped robes.

"Hello?" she tried to speak with one when it buzzed by, but it ignored her completely, focused instead on its work with the flowers.

"It won't answer you," said a voice behind her. "Not because it can't hear you or understand what you say, but it thinks what it's doing is more important, that's all."

Kitty turned around to see the old hag. She still had her red shawl around her but this time, she was wearing a bonnet on her head. Its once bright blue was faded and the edges had frayed. White wisps of her hair poked out from beneath it.

"Oh, hello," said Kitty turning around to face the old hag. "I need to read this book, only… well, I can't quite seem… what I mean is, I think it needs to be opened somehow so that it can be read as it really is, not what's printed on the pages." Kitty suddenly felt stupid because her sentence made no sense at all.

"Many things are not what they seem." The old hag nodded in understanding.

Kitty got up, picked up the book and walked toward her. "What do you see?" she asked, thrusting the book in front of the old hag.

"A book."

"Yes, but what does it say when you look at it?" Kitty urged.

"Don't know, can't read." The old hag smiled kindly.

"This is useless!" Kitty stomped away in frustration.

One of the bumblebee fairies buzzed around her ear. Kitty backed away from it. Then another joined it, and another, and soon there was a small swarm of them buzzing around her head.

Kitty didn't want to swat the fairies, but she couldn't see where she was going.

She stumbled back and hit something with a hollow thud. The fairy-bees flew away as swiftly as they arrived, leaving Kitty standing in front of an old wooden door with a small brass knob. Not the door she had entered last time to look into the future. This door was on the other side of the fairy garden. This was the door to the past.

Kitty looked back to see the fairy bumblebees swarming happily on top of the sundial. She knew they were operating it for her. *It must work like a kind of switch.* Last time she had touched it by accident and been sucked into, well, another part of Fairyland. The part where the doors to the past and the future rooms could be opened.

Turning to face the door to the past, she turned the doorknob and opened the door. Nutmeg and Baby quickly followed her and together they stepped into a windy turret.

The curved walls were covered in clocks of every kind. A cuckoo clock with a bird on a spring dangled on the wall. Next to it hung an enormous round clock with roman numerals and metal hands. It reminded her of the clock at the train station. Her eyes fell on a massive brass clock as high as the ceiling with all of the cogs exposed.

None of them ticked.

Below her feet, the floor was patterned like a huge compass. At the center stood a sundial, much like the one outside. Kitty's brow creased. Surely the roof above would prevent the sun from reaching the sundial?

A sudden gust of wind whipped her hair around her face. She pulled it back and noticed an archway at the most northerly point. Wondering what might lay beyond, she walked toward it. Passing under the arch, she almost fell.

Kitty gasped and gripped the wall to steady herself, almost dropping the book, her heart thumped in her throat. It was a long way down. Beyond the archway was a steep drop. She risked another peek over the edge. It went so far down that the bottom was covered in mist.

Backing away from the horribly long drop, she tried to take it all in. "I wonder how this can help me read the book of magic?"

"No idea..." Nutmeg gazed around in awe.

Cold stone stopped her wandering any further. She turned and glanced down, realizing that she had backed into the sundial in the middle of the room.

Baby walked around its base and said, "It was a sundial outside that allowed you to open the doors to the past and the future, perhaps this sundial does something too…"

Kitty touched the surface of the sundial, the warmth of her hand leached away by the cold stone.

She heard something, like a switch being triggered, then she whirled around. A waterfall tumbled behind the archway to the north.

Cuckoo! Cuckoo! The bird in the cuckoo clock bounced in and out on its spring.

Kitty cocked her head to one side and studied the waterfall. Every now and again, it seemed to crackle. She peered closely and saw that odd pictures were flashing up on the waterfall. Appearing for only a moment and then gone with a crackle. Like an old TV with bad reception.

"I wonder…."

"Wonder what?" asked Nutmeg.

"Well, when I used the Seeingscope, I had to state my question out loud, perhaps this room works the same way."

"You mean the waterfall might work like the Seeingscope and give you an answer?" asked Baby.

"It might."

Kitty pulled herself up straight and chose her words carefully. "How do I read the book?" she said out loud.

The waterfall spluttered and crackled.

Bong! The grandfather clock chimed.

All at once, every clock in the room started ticking backward, the hands racing so fast they blurred before her eyes.

Enormous cogs creaked and turned on the brass clock.

Cuckoo! Cuckoo!

Bong! Bong! Bong!

The noise was deafening. Kitty put her hands over her ears. Then, just as suddenly as it had begun, it stopped.

The waterfall revealed an image of an old leather bound book being opened by an elderly man in a pointy purple hat covered with stars. She peered closer and the image rippled, it was not her book.

"Hmm, I need to be more specific with my question."

Holding the book in the crook of her arm so that she could read the entire title she said, "Show me how to unlock, How to be Witchy, Practical Magic for Everyday Enchantment by B. Witcher."

The waterfall rippled, the clocks chimed and their hands spun back in time.

The waterfall showed an old woman in a black dress. She was very thin with wild, curly gray hair that stuck out in all directions. She sat at a wooden desk with the book in front of her. Moving a sputtering candle to one side, she picked up a magic wand and waved it over the book saying, "North, south, east, west, practical magic is the best."

Strands of purple and gold light snaked out from the book and the magic wand forming a web of light so dense that Kitty couldn't see the old woman open the book. When the image vanished from the waterfall, Kitty had the feeling she had seen enough.

She put the book down on the floor. "I need a wand," she huffed. Feeling a bit defeated she stuffed her hands into her pockets.

Her left hand felt something twig-like. She pulled it out and held it up. It was the stick of licorice Dr. McKracken had given her after treating her boils with the antidote to wishes.

"Well, this is a book on practical magic, maybe I need to be practical."

Holding the twig like a magic wand, she waved it over the book while chanting, "North, south, east, west, practical magic is the best."

Nothing happened.

Then the book hiccupped.

Tiny sparkles of golden light belched out.

More followed and swirled from the cover like octopus tentacles. Purple smoke drifted from the end of her twig-wand. The purple and gold light met and began to dance, weaving themselves together between Kitty and the book.

The front cover of the book dissolved to reveal an intricate golden lock. The purple smoke from the twig-wand formed itself into a key and turned the lock. A hundred tiny golden leavers flipped up all at once and the latch released.

The book was unlocked.

Kitty turned to the first page. Then the next and the next. She flipped through the whole book. "No... no!"

"What is it? What's wrong?" asked Nutmeg.

"All of the pages are blank."

This couldn't be possible. She couldn't have gone through all this only to find the pages were blank.

"Where's the table of contents?" She flipped through the book again, unable to believe there was nothing on the pages.

Both cats leaned in to look for themselves.

The book rumbled and a table of contents appeared. "Ah!" Kitty smiled, understanding how the book worked. It responded to questions.

Still holding her twig aloft she cleared her throat and said, "Wishing wells." The pages rustled themselves out of her grasp. She grabbed the book to hold it steady. It trembled and then doubled in size, making her and the cats jump back. It flipped open to a page with a large W at the top. Hundreds of entries for wishing wells appeared listed in spidery blue ink.

She turned the page, the list of wishing well entries went on and on...

Kitty knew she needed to be more specific with her question.

"How do I close the wishing well in my basement?"

The book popped, spun and returned to its original size. Under W on the contents page was one entry—

Wishing Wells: How to Close

She flipped to the correct page. It was the last page in the book. At the top of the page in bold was the title, but underneath, there were no words, only an image.

A sketch of a gargoyle.

11 MIDSUMMER'S EVE

MIDSUMMER'S EVE arrived with an endless blue sky that carried the sun aloft like a flaming torch. Its golden rays seeped throughout the garden, glinting on purple sweet peas and silvery foliage that spilled over borders and onto the lawn. Adoring blue periwinkles encircled the statue of the bathing lady, dressing her in a skirt of flowers.

"So, where will you go looking for these gargoyles?" asked Roger, his tone unusually serious.

"Ah, well, we'll be at the Midsummer's Parade tonight in the city. And there're gargoyles on lots of buildings. I'm sure I'll find one," said Kitty.

"And when you find one?" asked Nutmeg. "Then what? Gargoyles are not known for their animated conversation."

"I do hear they're great at karaoke, although I've never heard one so much as hum," said Roger.

Kitty and other two cats stared at Rodger. "What?"

Kitty sighed. "I'll have to corner a gargoyle somehow and, I don't know, keeping nagging until it talks?"

Nutmeg shook his head and Kitty snapped, "Well, what do you suggest?"

"The book showed you a picture of a gargoyle. Maybe trust that when you meet one, you'll know?" Baby said, her voice unsure.

"Maybe just finding one that hasn't been snatched yet is the first step," said Kitty, looking out of her bedroom window. "But that's not the only thing on my mind."

Pulling the Timekeeper out on its chain, Kitty winced.

"What is it?" asked Baby.

"Ouch, it just gave me an electric shock." Stuffing the Timekeeper back under her shirt, Kitty shook her hands.

"What's wrong with you?" asked Nutmeg peering out of one eye.

"Pins and needles in my fingers." Kitty scowled at her hands. She reached for her water glass and the water inside it fizzed.

The cats exchanged glances.

"It's my twelfth birthday, at midnight actually," said Kitty. "The old hag said that on my twelfth birthday, my bindings would unravel *completely*. What does that mean?" She turned to face the three cats.

Nutmeg sprawled in a sun puddle on the floor. Baby and Roger lay draped across her bed.

"No idea," said Nutmeg. His pink nose twitched in agitation.

"Wait a minute. If your bindings will unravel *completely*, does that mean they have already unraveled a bit?" asked Roger.

"The old hag said they had started to unravel early," said Kitty. "When I first arrived, a soup spoon jumped out of my hand and removed some snails from around the door frame, tossing them into the garden. And I can use the Timekeeper and travel into Fairyland."

"And she can hear us," said Baby.

"Talking with animals is certifiably witchy, that's for sure," said Roger, stretching before rolling onto his back.

"I mean, what else can happen?" Kitty looked at them all.

Nutmeg lifted a paw over his face and groaned.

Baby looked worried.

"Well, you'll know by midnight," said Roger, yawning.

"Not helpful, Roger," said Baby.

"Just focus on finding a gargoyle," mumbled Nutmeg from under his paw.

It was still light when Kitty and her grandparents left the house.

"It won't get dark until close to midnight tonight." Grandpa closed the garden gate after Grandma and winked at Kitty. "We're so far north that during the summer, it feels like it barely gets dark at all."

Kitty nodded her head to show she was listening yet her gaze lingered on her hands. The pins and needles she had felt in her fingertips since lunchtime were growing. Pushing that thought aside, a smile slid across her face, she was altogether too excited about the Midsummer's Eve Parade to worry about her bindings unraveling.

Grandpa said they had sword swallowers and fire breathers, troops of elves and a parade of giants. She could hardly wait. All thoughts of the crypt, the skeletons and the police hunt for the library burglar were gone from her mind.

Nothing could ruin this night.

"Are you walking into town for the Midsummer's Parade?" asked a snooty voice behind them. "So are we, why don't we join you?" It was a statement, not a question. "Children, come along."

Kitty's heart sank. No! Not the Snodgrasses, anybody but them.

"How wonderful." Grandpa turned to face Mrs. Snodgrass and smiled. "Please do join us. Is Mr. Snodgrass with you?"

"Sadly no, he is away on business. Marcus, Emily and I manage to struggle along without him." Mrs. Snodgrass smiled a fake smile.

Marcus and Emily appeared behind her. Marcus looked sullen and wicked at the same time. Like he had a nasty trick up his sleeve that no one knew about.

Emily, on the other hand, danced out of their garden singing in an awful off-key. "I'm a pink princess! I'm a pink princess!" She twirled clumsily out of the front gate in a ballerina's outfit with a ridiculous pink tutu and sequined shorts underneath. The tutu stuck straight out so everyone could see her shorts, which looked to Kitty to be a size too small. Emily seemed to know this and like it. She stopped her twirls every now and again to stick her bottom out and do some strange jerky move.

Kitty rolled her eyes.

Grandpa reached for her hand and gave it a reassuring squeeze. "Don't worry," he whispered in her ear. "It will be crowded at the parade, and you know how easy it is to get separated in a crowd."

Letting a smile tug at the corners of her mouth, Kitty and her Grandpa led the group on the short walk from the village of Dribble into the City of Edinburgh where the parade was held.

They didn't get far before running into a commotion on Hornblower Street. Police lights flashed on a recently arrived patrol car. A woman was screaming hysterically in her front garden. Kitty strained to hear what she was saying.

"I tell you, there were little hairy men in my pantry! The place is a mess and there is food everywhere! They ate my apple pie, they ate it! Laughed and ran away..." The woman broke down and sobbed on her own doorstep.

They kept walking and Kitty couldn't hear anymore after that. She looked ahead and further up the street, another two police officers were walking down a garden path toward a second patrol car. The front garden of the house was full of stuff—clothes, toys, furniture—like someone had thrown it all out of an upstairs window.

Grandpa's brow wrinkled. When they reached the police officers they were getting into their car. "Evening officers," said Grandpa. "Is everything ok? Two upsets on one street, very unusual for the village ..." He let his words trail off.

"I don't think there's anything to worry about sir," said the older of the two officers. "Something about little hairy men stealing food and making a mess. Probably just kids playing a prank if you ask me. It's the third call like this tonight—"

A shrill scream rang out in the next street. Kitty froze, wide eyed. The younger officer looked warily from side to side. "It's the Midsummer's Eve festival tonight, probably just revelers getting in the mood," he said with a sigh.

"Most likely," said Grandpa, looking around. "You are going to check that scream out though?"

"Of course sir, right away!" said the younger of the two.

Kitty's heart pounded while they continued down the street toward the parade. She knew it wasn't revelers or kids. She knew that scream belonged to a night stealer. And that the little hairy men were very real.

Nutmeg warned her they would wake up hungry and mischievous. All this mayhem was her fault. She swallowed hard, her mouth felt dry. But what could she do?

As they walked, her resolve to do something helpful hardened. She thought back to her conversation with the cats earlier. She must find a gargoyle. Somehow… But what if she couldn't? Well, she mused, at least she could talk to Grandpa, maybe find out more about the wishing well or what secrets lay behind the forbidden door in the basement. Without Grandma close by to stop him, he might let something slip.

Walking past a graveyard, the flagstones turned to cobbles underfoot. Kitty peered through a tall iron gate. It was ajar and she could see that the gravestones beyond stuck out at different angles like wonky teeth. She felt a chill and rushed to catch up with Grandpa.

Once they were out of earshot of the others she blurted out, "Grandpa, you know that room at the back of the basement, the one with the padlock on the door?"

"Yes."

"Well, I know you said I shouldn't worry about it, but I'm curious, what's in there?"

Grandpa sighed. "It's dark and cool in that back room. I use it for storing bottles of wine."

"But there's more to it than that, isn't there?"

Grandpa seemed to think about this for a moment, before replying. "You're growing up fast Kitty. Too fast for your old Grandpa," he said with a chuckle.

"Tell me Grandpa," Kitty said seriously.

"Yes. You'll be twelve in a few hours. I suppose you're old enough to know."

"Know what?"

"A long time ago, we, Grandma and I, together with Dr. McKracken, were all very good friends with another neighbor, Beatrice Witcher. She lived beside the library."

Kitty felt her fingers tingle at the mention of Beatrice

Witcher's name. She clenched them into fists by her side.

"Beatrice had a sense for things," Grandpa continued.

"Like what?"

"Well, she knew when it was going to rain. She would turn up at our house on a cloudless summer day with an umbrella and we knew that before teatime, there'd be a downpour. She was never wrong." Grandpa smiled and seemed far away for a moment. "And she had an uncanny knack for stopping bad things from happening. One time she called us on the phone and told us to check our kitchen right away. Well, Grandma had forgotten to turn off a pan on the stove and it was on fire. Another few minutes and the house would have been in flames." He chuckled and then his expression turned serious. "Don't mention that story to your Grandma."

"Course not." Kitty grinned. After a moment she asked, "But what does this have to do with the room in the basement?"

"Ah, Beatrice always said she didn't like that room. She was convinced that the old Penny Well was under the floor."

"Is it?"

"Not that we can see, nothing above ground anyway. I suppose it's possible that the old pit shaft that was drilled down into the ground is under the floor. It may even have water in it. We have had a couple of rather strange floods. The water seems to just bubble up out of the floor…"

"What else did Beatrice say?" Kitty asked.

"She said the old well was full of wild magic—"

"I thought you didn't believe in magic," Kitty interrupted.

"I don't, and I thought it was all nonsense of course. Strangely enough, after her…" Grandpa choked on his words. "She left us a rather unusual item. The axe at the bottom of the basement stairs. She also left strict instructions that the room be padlocked and the axe hung on the wall outside."

"So that's why the axe is there!"

"We thought it was all very strange, but then so was Beatrice." Grandpa chuckled to himself. "She really was quite eccentric. I think you would have liked her." He smiled at Kitty. "So, although it was a strange request, we honored it."

"Do you think the old Penny Well is under the floor?" Kitty asked.

"Perhaps, our house was built hundreds of years ago. It's possible the builders removed the pump and any anything above ground and simply covered over the pit shaft full of water."

"And then when it rains a lot—like it has this summer—the well shaft overflows and floods!" Kitty said, piecing the information together.

"Very possible," said Grandpa as they drew closer to Edinburgh.

"I really like the sound of your friend Beatrice, can I meet her?"

Grandpa's face turned grave. "I'm afraid not," he said.

"Why?"

He paused before answering. "We haven't seen her in a very long time."

Kitty got the feeling he was hiding something. "Where is she?"

Grandpa sighed. "She, err, disappeared many years ago."

"Disappeared? How does someone just disappear? I mean, what happened?"

"No one could be sure. However, one morning her house keys were found lying on the ground, but we never saw Beatrice again."

"How do you know she didn't just drop them?"

"Oh, I think we are almost there, look." Grandpa pointed to a crowd of people.

Instantly, Kitty forget all about Beatrice. She could hear the sounds of a carnival in full swing. Drums pounded and people cheered and laughed. As they walked closer to the center of town, the sounds grew louder and the crowds of people began to thicken.

"The parade runs down the Royal Mile, the main street of Edinburgh's old town," said Grandpa.

A man dressed like a devil ran past laughing and waving his pitchfork at them, his red rubber forked tail bounced behind him. He was joined by a giggling fairy in a shimmering green dress and silver wings.

"People love to dress up for this event," said Grandma from behind when a beautiful angel with long red hair walked past them. Her white feathery wings were so long that they trailed along the cobblestones. "Some of their costumes are quite convincing!"

The angel smiled and nodded at Grandma.

"I'm a pink princess! I'm a pink princess!" screeched Emily.

Kitty huffed. The quicker they escaped from the Snodgrass family the better.

"I'm beautiful too!" Emily whined.

"Of course you are my love, you are the most beautiful of them all," Mrs. Snodgrass crooned. "The most beautiful ballerina—"

"I'm not a ballerina, I'm a pink princess," Emily pouted. "Don't ever call me a ballerina again!" She stamped her pink frilly feet on the cobbles.

"No darling, I'm so sorry, my beautiful pink princess."

Kitty thought she was going to puke.

Emily marched ahead to catch up with Kitty, her arms crossed over her chest. "Kitty, what did you come as? You know, you're supposed to be in fancy dress. Well?" Her sparkly pink headband fell down over her eyes.

"I came as myself," said Kitty, not even looking at Emily.

"Well that's just stupid. Mummy, tell her that's just stupid." Emily tried to fix her headband but only managed to make her hair stick up like a spike on top of her head.

"Well, dear, everyone can dress up as whatever they want and—"

"Quite right," Grandpa interrupted, "we can all dress however we want."

Emily's face went red and screwed up like a dried out tomato. The spike of hair flopped to one side like a droopy stalk.

"And Emily, your outfit suits you quite perfectly," Grandpa said with a smile.

Kitty snorted, trying not to laugh. Grandpa was so good at telling people off without them even realizing it.

"I'm a pink princess!" Emily danced her way back to her mother, pirouetting and stumbling through the cobbles.

Realizing that she hadn't heard a word from Marcus since leaving their home, Kitty risked a glance back to see if he was still there. He walked beside his mother, looking quite bored too. He noticed Kitty watching him and his face broke into an evil grin. Kitty turned quickly away. What was going on? It was as if he knew something she didn't, something nasty. Another reason to get rid of the Snodgrasses and fast.

They turned onto Edinburgh's Royal Mile, the main street in the city, and Kitty almost bumped into a man on stilts. "Sorry!" She stumbled back. The ten-foot-tall man bowed politely to her, his clown makeup painted his mouth in a permanent grin. He stalked off down the street, his huge strides towering above the crowd.

Fire caught Kitty's eye. A juggler tossed burning torches into the air. She moved to the front of the crowd gathered around him for a better look. A man on a unicycle wearing a gold suit and top hat cycled in front of them while balancing a spoon on the end of his nose.

The sound of a saxophone drifted through the dusky summer air.

A group of people dressed like trees walked by, one by one they turned to look in Kitty's direction. She glanced behind her, expecting to see someone in an amazing costume standing there. But there was no one there but her grandparents. A prickle of fear ran up her spine. The tree people continued to stare at her. There was something wrong with the look on their faces.

"I'm going to be in the parade!" Emily jumped in front of her, cutting Kitty's eye contact with the strange tree men. "My mum knows the people in charge you see."

She did some fluttery movements that Kitty supposed must be dancing.

"We're important people. We know important people." Emily prattled on. "Who do you know that's important?" Her nasty little face bunched up so that she looked like a hairless hamster. And then she fell over.

Or more precisely, was knocked over by what looked like a little hairy man.

At first Kitty started to laugh, thinking this must be someone in fancy dress. That'll wipe that smile off her face, Kitty thought. And then she got a closer look at what pushed Emily down. The thing got up, looked up at Kitty, and bared its needle sharp teeth before running away.

Kitty's blood froze. It must be a night stealer. And it was here, at the parade, among thousands and thousands of people. Kitty's mind raced, what could she do?

"Mummy! Mummy!" Emily wailed. "Kitty pushed me over!"

"I did not!" Kitty couldn't believe it. She wasn't even that close to Emily when it happened. Didn't anyone else see? She looked around for her grandparents and saw them both spellbound by a fire-breathing man in a Godzilla suit.

"My poor little princess!" Mrs. Snodgrass rushed to Emily's side.

Hearing the commotion, Grandpa turned around. "Everything alright?"

"No, your granddaughter has just attacked my Emily. Again!"

"I didn't!"

"Now, now, there are a lot of people here, there is always some pushing and shoving in crowds. I am sure it was just an accident, nothing more. Emily, can you walk?" Grandpa walked over to Emily and helped her up. "I think you're made of stronger stuff that that," he said, pinching her cheek and smiling.

"Emily sniffed, "I'm going to be in the parade because I'm important."

"Wonderful!" said Grandpa. "We're all looking forward to seeing you dance down the street," he said, his smile never faltering.

Kitty was seething and her hands tingled. That horrid little girl had just blamed her for something she hadn't done—and been believed—again. And she was in the parade. Kitty hated to admit it, but she was just a little bit jealous.

The tingling in her fingertips became pins and needles, encompassing her whole hand.

"Look now." Grandpa pointed at the Cathedral ahead. "There's a witch trial going on, let's go and take a peek." He led their whole group toward a cobbled square outside St. Giles' Cathedral where a reenactment of a witch trial was in full swing.

"Not the only trial there's going to be," Marcus hissed in Kitty's ear as he walked by.

Kitty was still trying to figure out what Marcus meant when they reached the witch trial. Hundreds of grinning skulls lit with candles surrounded the performance area. A man standing on top of a huge stone podium read out the charges.

"I'm innocent! I did nothing wrong! Just used a few herbs to help the sick!" the witch on trial pleaded.

Several other actors, meant to be judges and police officers, scoffed and jeered. And then they started chanting. "Burn the witch! Burn the witch! Burn the witch!" The crowd of spectators joined in.

The judge carried a flaming torch to light the pyre where the witch would burn, but before he reached it, he turned toward the crowd of spectators. He was staring straight at Kitty with a crazy look in his eyes as he chanted, "Burn the witch! Burn the witch! Burn the witch!"

Some people in the crowd started to look at her too while they joined in the chant.

"Burn the witch! Burn the witch!"

Kitty stumbled backward.

"Burn the witch! Burn the witch!"

"Well, that's enough here, let's move along." Grandpa moved them all down the street, away from the witch trials.

He did so effortlessly and everyone followed him without question. It amazed Kitty how he did that. How did he get people to do what he wanted without even trying? She made a mental note to ask him about it later.

Right now, she was too freaked out with all of the strange people staring at her and chanting. What did any of that have to do with her? And what did Marcus mean about another trial? And what about the night stealers?

A painful riving at her neck brought Kitty out of her thoughts.

Something was choking her!

Her hand grasped instinctively around her throat as the silver chain on which the Timekeeper dangled was pulled over her head.

"I got your necklace! I got your necklace!" chanted Emily, dangling it in front of Kitty's face.

"Give that back!" Kitty grabbed for it as Emily pulled it away, skipping about in her pink tutu.

"Emily." Kitty held out her hand and in her most grown-up voice said, "Give it back, now."

"No." Emily screwed up her face.

Kitty glanced around for her grandparents and found them only a few feet in front with their backs to her, watching a man swallow a sword.

Emily turned around to see what Kitty was looking at.

While she was distracted, Kitty took her chance and grabbed for the Timekeeper. But Emily did not let go of the chain.

"Give it back!" Kitty yelled.

Kitty gaped at her outstretched palm and was shocked to see blue sparks of light dancing down to her fingertips. She clenched her hands into fists before Emily noticed.

What was going on? If this was her magical bindings unraveling *completely*, Kitty didn't like it.

"Ladies, please!" Mr. Wolf appeared next to them, jovial as always. "I am sure there is a way to sort this out."

Kitty took a deep breath. "Emily stole my necklace and refuses to give it back."

"Did not!"

"Yes, you did!"

"It's mine and Kitty pushed me over!"

"Dear me Emily, are you alright?"

Kitty rolled her eyes in disgust. Surely he wasn't going to fall for Emily's lies.

Mr. Wolf moved between them, comforting Emily who lapped up the attention.

Kitty huffed and crossed her arms.

Next thing Kitty knew, Mr. Wolf had somehow wrestled the Timekeeper from Emily's grasp and winked at Kitty while handing it back to her.

Kitty couldn't help but smile. She opened her hand to receive the Timekeeper. The blue sparks of light that had danced on her fingertips a moment ago, were gone.

"Ah, I see your family just ahead," said Mr. Wolf guiding Emily to where her mother and brother stood.

Kitty put the Timekeeper back around her neck and followed along, peering up at the old buildings.

"Looking for the gargoyles?" Mr. Wolf asked.

"How did you know?"

"The news is full of stories of their disappearance, everyone is talking about it," Mr. Wolf replied with a nod. "I must admit, I keep hoping for a glimpse myself." He gazed up wistfully. "Sadly, I am yet to see one."

Things were a little quieter on the other side of St. Giles'

Cathedral. Mrs. Snodgrass had made a beeline for Grandpa, determined to establish Kitty's guilt in pushing Emily down in the street earlier.

While Grandpa and Grandma were busy calming Mrs. Snodgrass down and Emily was busy spinning around in a circle and singing off key, Marcus swaggered over to Kitty.

"So, get anything nice for your birthday?" He pushed her into a doorway where no one could see them.

"What?"

Kitty felt the rough wood of an old door against her back and Marcus's warm breath on her face. It didn't smell nice.

"Dog breath!" She squirmed away from him.

"How about some of your birthday money in exchange for me getting you the key to the library," he said.

"That wasn't our deal!" Kitty was both angry and confused. "We agreed to exchange keys—I gave you the key to the summerhouse, you gave me the key to the library."

"I'll bet there's birthday money in these pockets." Marcus moved in and thrust his hand into her jeans pocket. "And if I don't get some I'm going to tell the police that I saw you running from the library at the time of the break-in."

Kitty kicked out of instinct. Her foot slammed into the inside of his knee and Marcus crumpled like a rag doll. Before he could recover, Kitty was out of the doorway and back on the crowded street. Like a piece of driftwood at high tide, Kitty was swept away in a sea of people.

12 MISSING GARGOYLES

THE CROWD rumbled down the Royal Mile carrying Kitty with them. She was so mad with Marcus she thought her head might blow off. How dare he rifle through her pockets? *How dare he?* And his breath, ugh!

Still raging, she looked around for her grandparents. Being shorter than most of the crowd she couldn't see much other than cobbles under her feet. She took a deep breath, *I need get out of this crowd.*

A space opened up to her left and Kitty pushed through the gap, tumbling into a dimly lit alleyway. Stone buildings rose up to either side of her. Trailing down the narrow path, she passed under an ancient archway and found herself on a deserted road. From behind her she could make out the distant sounds of the parade. A shadow skittered across her path making her jump.

The tree men stood at the far mouth of the alley. The same men in incredibly realistic tree costumes who had glared at her earlier. She would have to walk past them to get back to the parade. Kitty bit her lip, wishing she had stayed in the crowd.

She looked right to a sign high up on the side of a building that read, Fleshmarket Close. A figure stood beneath it wearing a dark costume with a long sharp beak and a hooded cloak. Kitty was sure he wasn't there a moment before. The sharp beak turned toward her. Although she couldn't see his eyes, she felt he was watching her.

She glanced back. The tree men were still there. Was it her imagination or had they moved closer? Heart pounding, Kitty turned left and started to walk down the cobbled bank, away from the birdman and the menacing tree people.

Footsteps grew louder behind her.

Her fingers started to tingle. Oh no, not the blue sparks again.

"It's her!"

Kitty looked up and saw figures coming up the bank on the way to her.

Her only exit was blocked.

Kitty fisted her hands to stop them shaking. *Who are they? What do they want?*

Her eyes searched the darkened street for an escape.

Stone steps descended to her left. They were so narrow she could touch the walls on either side, but they were open to the night sky above. She ran down them toward a light. The thud of her feet echoed off the ancient stone. The light she was running to suddenly went out, blocked by a huge shadow.

She stopped dead.

Someone sniggered in the darkness just ahead of her.

Pins and needles shot down from her palms to her fingertips. Peeking over her shoulder, she saw the bird man and tree people stood at the top of the stairs. The gathering mob stared down at her.

She was trapped.

"Who are you? What do you want with me?" she called out. Frantically her eyes scanned the walls to either side. There, on the right, about five steps down, barely visible against the stone, was a small wooden door.

The wood was blackened with dirt and age, Kitty would have never seen it if it weren't for the shiny new padlock glinting in the moonlight.

The shadow moved closer. Keeping her back to the wall, Kitty inched a few steps lower. Her hand gripped over the padlock and crackling blue light escaped her fingers.

The door creaked open an inch, but the padlock held fast. The door was so old, it had rotted around the hinges.

"Going somewhere?" the shadowy figure rasped. Stepping out of the shadows, he lunged at her.

Kitty thrust out her hands in self-defense, only to see them engulfed in blue crackling flame. An arc of light shot from her fingertips toward the figure in front of her, but instead of pushing him away, it backfired and slammed her whole body backward.

The old wooden door gave way with a splintering groan. Falling back she fell on her butt, scurried to her feet and spun around, finding herself in a narrow passageway.

Every sense in her body tingled. She heard scratching sounds ahead, followed by angry shouts from behind. She moved forward blindly with her hands outstretched. The stonework was rougher here, not smooth like the side of the buildings flanking the stairway she had just left.

A howl rang out behind her and the remains of the door splintered as her pursers forced their way through.

Groping her way around the rough walls, Kitty nearly fell when the passageway sloped suddenly downward. The air grew colder and she realized she must be winding her way beneath the city.

If only I had some light.

Then she remembered the tiny flashlight on her keyring. She fumbled through her pockets and flicked it on. A weak blue light cast eerie shadows onto rough stone walls. It smelled musty and ducking under a low archway, she could hear the scurrying of rats ahead.

I wish Grandpa was here.

Thinking of him made her remember something he had said. Part of Edinburgh's Old Town was built on top of existing buildings which were used as foundations—just like the library was built on top of the old church.

Kitty realized that she must be under the city, in what Grandpa had called the catacombs. But how would she get out? She couldn't risk going back the way she had come.

Just then, she heard the sound of boots scraping stone, followed by a muffled curse of someone tripping. She stood still and silent. The voices and footsteps were getting closer.

The mob!

She stumbled on, holding her tiny flashlight above her, following its dim light deeper and deeper into the catacombs.

A dark shape scuttled in front of her, Kitty jumped. It was too large to be a rat and it ran upright on two legs. Her heart sank, not the night stealers, not down here! Biting her lip, she peered cautiously into the darkness ahead.

Two eyes stared back. Taking a hesitant step closer, her small light fell on large, pointy ears that rested upon a bald, rock-like head. It was no night stealer.

Kitty edged closer, the creature backed away into the darkness. "Hello?" Kitty called after it. "I'm not going to hurt you. I just need to find a way out of here. Can you help me?"

Footsteps clumped along the passageway behind her. The voices of the mob were clearer now. They were close. "Come along little girl," one of them sneered. "We're not going to hurt you." Sniggers and evil laughter echoed around the catacombs.

Kitty felt a small tug on her jeans and looked down to see the rock-like creature take off into the darkness. She dashed after it, down a long corridor, around a corner and skidded straight into a wall. Her worst fear. A dead end.

She spun around intending to go back the way she had come, but the way was blocked. The birdman stood there, his beak open in an unmistakable leer.

"Leaving so soon?" he jeered. "But we've just got here." He held up a lantern.

Kitty's mind raced as she backed away, right into the dead end.

"I am disappointed you want to leave." The birdman took a step forward. "Which is of little consequence. My master, however, will also be disappointed, and the consequences of disappointing him are, how can I put it? Unpleasant."

The master he spoke of could only be one person. The bogeyman.

The birdman held up the lantern. Wicked shadows cast by his long-beaked mask bounced off the walls. The mob bobbed about excitedly.

"He's here!" hissed a voice behind the birdman. The mob parted to let someone through. A shadow settled over Kitty.

Her legs went wobbly and her teeth began to chatter. In her hand the flashlight flickered.

The owner of the shadow moved closer.

Kitty gasped as the most beautiful music filled the room. She had never heard angels sing, but if she could ever describe angel song, this would be it. Each note slid like silk across a harp string and rose up in waves that crashed against the walls of the catacombs in a melodious strum.

Suddenly, the mob in front of her crumpled to their knees, screaming, their hands pressed over their ears. The birdman dropped his lantern, smashing it and plunging them into darkness.

A small, rough hand slipped into hers and tugged, urging her to follow. Kitty looked down and onto the same pointy eared, broad-faced creature she had followed a few moments ago. Without a word, she let the creature lead her away.

An archway opened up in the wall to her left, an opening that wasn't there before. Although the creature could walk through at its full height without stooping, Kitty had to crouch low to get through. Once on the other side, the music stopped. Stone grated on stone and Kitty turned around to see the archway disappear as if it had never been there.

Candles filled the room and illuminated a dozen or so statues of various sizes. Kitty squinted to see what they were. Some kind of animals, she thought at first.

The creature at her side squeezed her hand. Kitty glanced down into its smiling face. She knew she should feel afraid, but she didn't. She felt safe. Not only safe, but happy. Like Christmas morning and going on a trip and getting a snow day off school, all rolled into one.

Looking up, she saw the largest of the statues blink, candlelight reflecting off big purple eyes.

It moved slowly toward Kitty, weaving around the other statues and candles. As it came nearer, Kitty could make out its shape. It had the body of a lion, although it walked upright, the wings of a bird, a long snout with big round nostrils, almond shaped eyes, pointy ears and horns. Its hind claws scraped the stone floor as it walked toward her.

"Good evening Kitty Tweddle," it said in a crackly voice. "My name is Zebulon and I am the last gargoyle."

Zebulon's stony features were covered with lichens. A patch of green moss grew on his head like a toupee. He squinted at her, his long snout almost touching her nose before reaching into some hidden pocket about his person and producing a pair of round spectacles. "You must excuse me, my eyesight is not what it used to be." He chuckled and put the spectacles on, blinking his purple eyes. "Now, step into the light please, let's take a good look at you."

Kitty stepped forward and Zebulon stepped back. The candlelight glinted off the green moss on Zebulon's head making it sparkle. It reminded Kitty of the fairy garden she had seen through Dr. McKracken's Revealer. His mossy hair looked as if it had a life of its own.

"You're a... a real gargoyle?"

"I am."

"Gargoyles have the power to ward off evil don't they?" asked Kitty.

"Indeed." Zebulon adjusted his stance.

Some of the other statues started to move.

"A few moments ago, on the other side of that wall, the mob that was chasing you fell to its knees in agony and terror. Tell me, Kitty, what did you hear?" The other creatures in the room moved closer.

"I heard the most beautiful singing I have ever heard in my entire life," Kitty answered. "It sounded like the voices of angels."

Zebulon clasped his paws in front of his puffed-out chest and nodded. "Do you know what they heard?"

"No."

"They heard the most terrifying, blood-curdling screams, like a horde of demons coming to tear them limb from limb. Do you know why?"

"No."

"Because they are evil, and as gargoyles it is our job to ward off evil. Only those who are pure of heart can hear our song as it truly is."

"So, you do have the voices of angels?"

"No, we have the voices of gargoyles. Those throughout history who have heard us sing have assumed that voices so beautiful could not belong to ugly gargoyles, and must belong to the angels. As a matter of fact," he said, raising an eyebrow and leaning in as if to tell her a secret. "Angels are not very good singers. Fantastic musicians mind you. Quite marvelous with brass and strings."

The little creature at Kitty's side bent its head in toward her, still holding her hand.

"I see you have met Holly the hunkey punk." Zebulon nodded.

"Holly the what?"

"Hunkey Punk."

Kitty looked down at Holly. "Isn't she a gargoyle like you and the rest?"

"No, I am the last gargoyle. My colleagues here are all hunkey punks."

"What's a hunkey punk and how are they different from gargoyles?"

"Allow me to explain." Zebulon peered over the top of his spectacles. "A gargoyle is only a gargoyle if he or she funct-ions as a water spout." He turned around to reveal a deep groove running the length of his back in between his wings.

"It looks a bit… rusty…" Kitty grimaced.

"Sadly, an iron pipe was installed early in the last century. None of my colleagues here has such a spout, they are all, how can I put it, ornamental. For show. They do not function as water spouts, they do not channel water away from the building they perch upon. Many do not perch at all, but sit in gardens rather like gnomes."

Several hunkey punks turned around to show their spoutless backs.

"However, because people believe we are the same thing and have the same power, to ward off evil, we can all do it. We all have, how did you put it? Angel song."

The other hunkey punks nodded in agreement.

"Belief is both a marvelous and a terrible thing. Belief makes things real."

Remembering the news reports about the missing gargoyles, Kitty decided to ask Zebulon about it. "I heard on the news that someone is taking the city's gargoyles."

"That's right. Taken by the one we call, the bogeyman."

"The bogeyman?" Kitty repeated.

Zebulon took a deep breath, considering his next words. "Two of my operatives and dear friends attempted to contact you when you arrived in the city. They followed your taxi. They were trying to warn you of the danger you are in when they too, were... taken." Zebulon sniffed.

"I remember! I saw something flying behind the taxi and then it was gone," Kitty's voice trailed off.

"Indeed, one minute a gargoyle is there, the next, poof! We do not know how he does it, but that is neither here nor there. Our pressing problem is that we know something magical is happening in the basement of your house. We suspect an old wishing well may be the culprit."

"Yes, it's in the basement. Dr. McKracken says it's the old

Penny Well from the convent from hundreds of years ago. Even my Grandpa, who doesn't believe in magic, thinks there may be an old well under the floor."

"I am afraid I must ask you some rather personal questions." Zebulon looked embarrassed. "Have you made any wishes?"

"Wishes? No. But I have been on the receiving end of some very old ones." Kitty sighed and decided she had better explain to Zebulon. "I picked up a penny I found and got a face full of boils, and then I fell on another one and got the most ridiculous hair you have ever seen in your life!"

"So, the old coins that people threw into the wishing well hundreds of years ago have surfaced, bringing the old wishes with them. That must be how the bogeyman found his way back into this world. Through the wishing well."

"How?"

"How indeed." Zebulon took a moment to consider his next words. "How do beings from Fairyland enter our world? First, they must have an entry point. A place where the barrier between the two words is thin and easy to cross over. A magical place, like a wishing well."

"But the wishing well has been there for centuries, why is he coming now?"

"Excellent question." Zebulon raised an eyebrow. "Even with a magical portal, like a wishing well, there are only two ways a being like the bogeyman can enter this world. Either, he must be invited by someone here, or..."

"Or?" Kitty urged.

"Or, he must break the rules."

"What rules and how could he break them?" Kitty asked.

"The rules are older than time itself and found in all cultures around the world. No being can enter this world from another realm without being invited. Of course, some people invite beasts like the bogeyman unwittingly."

"How would someone break the rules and open a doorway to Fairyland without knowing it?"

"Dark things… Terrible deeds…" Zebulon clasped his paws. "There are two ways someone might open a portal to the fairy realm unintentionally. The first, and most unforgivable, is the commission of an evil act, like murder." Zebulon let his words hang in the air. "The taking of another life wrenches the doorway open."

"I think I might know who, my Grandpa's friend Beatrice disappeared a long time ago. She told my Grandpa that the well under the floor in the forbidden room was filled with wild magic."

"I believe that is correct." Zebulon nodded. "The second way, is if a human comes into contact with a cursed object. Like a bad penny from a wishing well perhaps? This may also have acted as an invitation for the bogeyman to cross over into this world, or strengthened him if he was already here."

"Oh no…" Kitty hung her head, knowing that she had touched such an object. A bad penny cursed with a wicked wish.

Kitty was silent for a moment. Before coming to her grandparents' house, Kitty hadn't really believed in wishes, bogeymen or magic.

"Be careful what you wish for Kitty Tweddle, because wishes can come true," said Zebulon. "My only other question is… Why have you not closed down the wishing well? After all, it is in your house."

"Me? I don't know how!"

Murmurs rattled around the room.

"You do not know how? Gracious me, then this is worse

than I thought." Zebulon stared off into the darkness, lost in thought.

"I have the book, the book of magic," Kitty blurted out. "And when I asked it how to close down the wishing well, it showed me a picture of a gargoyle. I was hoping you could do it."

"I see..." Zebulon turned back to face Kitty, his brow creased as he considered this. "It would appear that our paths are intertwined on this journey. We must work together to close down this old wishing well and banish the bogeyman back to the fairy realm."

A clock chimed at the back of the room. A small hunkey punk with a clock embedded in his chest came forward. "It's midnight," he whispered to Zebulon before looking sheepishly at Kitty. "I have a clock," he said pointing to his chest.

"I can see that." Kitty grinned.

"Happy Birthday Kitty Tweddle," said Zebulon.

"Thank you! I had completely forgotten about my birthday..."

"I sense the last of your magical bindings has released, do you feel any different?"

"Well," Kitty paused to look down at her hands. "The pins and needles in my fingers have stopped."

"Good. Well, I believe it is time we got you home. How do you feel about flying?"

Kitty didn't have time to respond.

Zebulon walked toward the back of the room, waved a paw in front of the wall and a doorway appeared. "Follow me please."

Zebulon fluttered up a flight of steps, through a door and out into a deserted courtyard with Kitty following behind.

"You had better hang on."

Kitty reached her arms around Zebulon's shoulders and he took off with a great flap of his wings.

"Agh!" Kitty let out a scream of surprise and clung firmly to the flying gargoyle. For a moment she squeezed her eyes tight shut, the breeze whipping through her hair and filling her nostrils.

"I love flying!" Zebulon roared as he swooped left, flying over the crowd milling down the Royal Mile.

Kitty opened her eyes and gasped as they glided above the rooftops. The people on the streets below looked like ants swarming on the town.

"Are you alright?" Zebulon asked.

"Yes, fine," Kitty said, starting to enjoy herself.

Zebulon laughed and soaring high, he looped around a church spire and dived toward a graveyard almost skimming the gravestones before banking steeply to exit through a deserted open gate.

He slowly descended and Kitty recognized her surroundings. Zebulon landed at the end of Kitty's street.

"Best if I let you walk from here," said Zebulon.

Kitty could see her grandparents' front door. "That was amazing! Thanks." She kissed his stony cheek before running toward the front gate of number five, Crescent Avenue.

Reaching the gate, she turned to wave goodbye, but Zebulon did not wave back.

He looked around, his purple eyes searching. His nostrils quivered, and his tail shuddered. He opened his mouth. Whether to sing or speak Kitty could not guess, because in the next instant, he disappeared with a *poof!*

13 THE PURPLE DOOR

"YOU'RE LUCKY I'm an early riser," said Roger as he padded softly up the narrow stairs behind Kitty. It was early morning and with her grandparents out at the market, Kitty grasped the opportunity to explore more of the secret passageways.

They passed the entrance to her Grandma's ballroom closet. "Nutmeg and Baby couldn't be ready this early. They can't leave the house in the morning until their humans let them," Roger continued. As a stray cat, he didn't have a home to be let out of. "Me? I'm always ready. I was born ready!"

"I bet you never even slept last night," Kitty said.

"Night tiiiiime is the right tiiiiiiime…" Roger broke into song.

"Right time for what?"

"Romancing the ladies of course! They can't get enough of me." Roger slunk ahead, weaving through Kitty's legs and almost tripping her up. "I am a star catch." Roger flopped down on the narrow landing ahead, rolled onto his side and let his generous belly spill onto the dusty floor.

The candle Kitty held aloft reflected eerily off his eyes.

Stepping over Roger, the narrow stairs creaked underfoot while she climbed. Brushing a cobweb aside, Kitty's eyes strained to see beyond the candlelight. Roger, of course, had no problems. "I wish I could see in the dark like you can." Kitty coughed with the dust as she reached the top of the stairs. The passageway twisted back on itself again.

"So, what did *you* do last night?" Roger asked, trotting ahead.

Kitty raced through the events of the previous night. Escaping Marcus, being chased by the mob, getting lost in the catacombs deep beneath the city and meeting the gargoyles.

"You found them? That's great! Are they going to fix this wishing well problem of yours then?" He turned around to face her.

"No. I mean they can't. I mean they don't know how."

"Typical," muttered Roger.

"And it's much worse than that. After Zebulon dropped me off, he disappeared right in front of me. He's gone Roger, and I don't know what to do," she sighed. "The gargoyles were my only hope of shutting down the wishing well and stopping the bogeyman, and now the last one is gone."

Kitty came to what appeared to be a dead end. She knew from her experience in these passageways that it couldn't be, as all of the other dead ends were actually well concealed doors. Surely this must be one too?

She held the candle up to the wall, looking for some edge or secret panel. She found none. The candle flickered close to the end of its stump. There would not be enough light to guide her way back if she didn't turn around soon. She tried pushing the wall in various places, just like she had done at the library, perhaps this doorway opened differently to the others? Nothing moved.

The candle sputtered.

"Ooh scary! Shall we tell ghost stories now?" said Roger, getting so close that his whiskers tickled her face.

"Not helping, Roger."

Nothing for it now, she thought, I have to get through this door. Taking a deep breath, she threw all her weight against the door and with a shriek of protest, the hinges gave way and she tumbled through.

She looked around in amazement. Dr. McKracken's attic study! These passageways did link the two houses together, just like the story her grandparents had told her.

Kitty sat up and faced the shelves of potion bottles and jars.

Roger padded through cautiously, sniffing the air.

The little doorway she had fallen through was almost concealed in the wood-paneling, so she hadn't noticed it last time she was here.

Sunlight streamed through the window illuminating bits of dust floating in the air. She stood up and almost tripped up over a pile of books. Picking her way through, she headed toward the desk and sat down.

"This place is a mess," said Roger.

Kitty looked around the room, there were papers and books scattered everywhere. "Dr. McKracken must be very busy researching something. But what?"

She leant against some papers sending them sliding all over the floor. Bending down to pick them up, she noticed a black leather-bound book on the desk. Silver stars and moons covered its surface. Putting the papers down, Kitty picked the book up, tracing the rough trough of a crescent with her finger.

"What's that?" asked Roger.

"I'm not sure, but it looks interesting…"

Kitty was about to open it when she saw something sticking out.

A photograph.

She pulled it out. It was a photograph of a woman holding a baby. It looked like it was taken in her grandparents' house. She flipped the photo over and studied the back. There, to her surprise, handwritten in spidery writing, were the words *Kitty Tweddle*. This must be a photograph of her as a baby. But who was the old woman holding her?

Footsteps clip-clopped up the stairs.

"Someone else is up early," said Roger, retreating back into the secret passageway in a flash. Kitty quickly turned toward the secret doorway which still stood wide open. She could see a small shelf inside with more candles and matches, just like all the other secret doorways.

I must remember my flashlight next time.

She ducked through the small doorway reaching for a candle before she closed the door behind her.

"Roger, no singing, please?"

Footsteps entered the attic room beyond. Kitty and Roger waited in the darkness, Kitty holding her breath, afraid the sound of her breathing would give her away.

Dr. McKracken—it must have been him—rustled around the papers on his desk, turned around and walked out of the room.

Kitty breathed a deep sigh of relief before groping around the dusty shelf and grabbing a box of matches. Holding the candle between her knees, she opened the matchbox, pulled out a match and struck it, lighting up the tiny space and almost setting Roger's whiskers on fire.

"Oye! Careful!"

"Keep your whiskers out of my face then!"

They moved quickly and quietly down the narrow steps all the way to her bedroom.

Kitty flopped on the bed. "I wonder who she is?" She pulled the photograph from her pocket and studied it.

Grandpa's footsteps thudded toward her room, followed by a brisk knock on her bedroom door.

"Kitty, come upstairs. Right away please."

She felt her stomach tighten. Grandpa's voice didn't sound very happy.

Pushing herself off the bed, she wondered which of the extraordinary events from the past few days could be the problem.

"I'll just wait here then," said Roger, slinking under the bed.

"Good idea," said Kitty.

When she arrived home last night her Grandma had just hugged her, relieved she was safe. Grandpa was still out searching for her with the local police, but neither seemed mad at her. After all, she did get lost in the crowd, it wasn't her fault. She had just kicked Marcus Snodgrass, but he did try to frisk her. Of course, she didn't tell her grandparents that part.

Did they know about the gargoyles? Had the night stealers caused more trouble?

Thoughts spun around her head as she wound her way up the stairs and into the kitchen. In front of her stood two police officers, her grandparents and a grinning Marcus Snodgrass.

"Kitty Tweddle, my name is Police Constable Burns and this—" He indicated to the woman to his left. "Is Constable McTavish from the Dribble police force. We are here to ask you some questions about a break-in at the village library two nights ago. Is there anything you would like to tell us?"

Kitty's mouth fell open like a gawping fish. She couldn't believe it. Marcus Snodgrass had actually reported her to the police for breaking into the library. He had threatened to do it last night if she didn't give him money, but she didn't believe he actually would. After all, they had exchanged keys. She had loaned him the key to the summerhouse while he had loaned her the key to the library.

How could she prove any of this? They had each returned the borrowed keys the next day. It was all so unfair!

"Kitty, don't you have anything to say to the police constable?" asked Grandma.

"Um... I didn't break in... exactly," Kitty stuttered. Her head was swimming, what could she say? That she had borrowed a key from Marcus Snodgrass to enter the library and borrow a book that was hidden in the crypt, and accidentally woken up some night stealers who were now causing mayhem?

"Damage was caused to the library Kitty, a window was broken, could you tell us anything about that?" Constable McTavish asked.

"I didn't break any windows," Kitty answered. And it was true, she hadn't. The night stealers had broken the windows when they escaped, but the police would never believe that.

Constable Burns sighed and turned to Marcus. "Can you please tell us what you reported to the police earlier this morning, Marcus?"

"It was her, I saw her running away from the library," he spat and then went back to looking pleased with himself.

"I wasn't aware you could see the library from next door Marcus," said Grandpa.

"You live next door? But you said you saw Kitty from your bedroom window? Can you explain how you witnessed Kitty leaving the library if your home is half a mile away?" asked Constable Burns.

Marcus turned a shade of pink and screwed up his face. "It was her!" was all he could say.

"I see..." said Constable Burns. "It looks like we have two culprits on our hands. No honor among thieves then!"

"It wasn't me!" shouted Marcus.

"Well you were certainly in the vicinity at the time of the crime," said Constable Burns. "And not in your home to have seen Kitty leaving, as you claim."

"Was anything stolen?" asked Grandpa.

"Not that we are aware of, although there is a lot of broken glass outside the library which is hazardous."

"The broken window glass is *outside* the library?"

"Those details are police business. Nothing for you to concern yourself with," said Constable Burns.

Ignoring him, Grandpa continued, "If the broken glass is outside, it suggests someone breaking out, not in."

"Yes, I agree sir, and that's what I said—"

"Like I said, that's police business," Constable Burns cut McTavish off.

Allowing the matter to drop, Grandpa scowled at Kitty. "Perhaps a call to your mother is in order."

"No!" wailed Kitty. She hung her head. "I was there," she admitted. "But I didn't break any windows, I swear!"

The two police officers exchanged knowing glances.

"In cases involving children, we usually ask the parents or guardians to pay for any damage and have the kids involved do community service as punishment. Any objections?" asked Constable Burns.

"No, none from us," said Grandpa.

"What? You're not going to tell my mother, are you?" Marcus's face had gone from pink to purple with rage.

"Yes we are, and because you asked, why don't we go and tell her right now." Constable Burns guided Marcus toward the door.

"Kids," Constable McTavish said and smiled reassuringly at Grandpa. "We often find that a good bit of community service and making them accountable for their actions works wonders," she said. "We've already talked it over with the head librarian and fortunately, he has agreed to the culprits helping out with some cleaning in the library grounds. They are to report to..." She flipped open a notebook. "Mr. Wolf at 7pm on Monday evening, when the library closes."

"Well, thanks for your time, we'll be getting along now." Constable McTavish followed Constable Burns and a protesting Marcus Snodgrass out of the door.

"Kitty, I think it might be best if you stay indoors for the rest of the day and have a think about what you have done." Grandma sounded like she wanted to cry.

Kitty hung her head and walked away, back down the stairs to her basement bedroom. She felt awful for letting her grandparents down. But what else could she do? They told her when she arrived that they didn't believe in magic. How could she explain a magic book, the bogeyman and the night stealers?

Walking into her bedroom, she heard scratching at the window. Opening the curtains, she saw Nutmeg's pink nosed, ginger face pushed up against the glass. She opened it and let him in. His paws left muddy prints on the windowsill.

"Morning," he grumbled.

"Morning," Kitty moaned.

"What's wrong with you?"

Kitty heaved a great sigh, flopping down onto the bed. She barely knew where to start.

Baby followed him and dropped to the floor in front of Kitty's bed. "Ouch!" Baby flinched and spun about as a giggling Roger crept out from his hiding spot.

"He just bit my tail!" Baby complained.

"Don't exaggerate, it was just a friendly nibble."

"Nibble!"

"Alright, alright." Nutmeg got between them. "I think we may have bigger problems." All three cats turned to face Kitty.

"I've been arrested by the police."

"What!" all three cats said at once.

Kitty told them the whole story, from the Midsummer's Parade, to Marcus Snodgrass threatening to report her to the police to being chased by an evil mob and being rescued by gargoyles.

"Wait, you found the gargoyles?" asked Nutmeg.

"I already knew this," said Roger with a smug look on his face.

"Shhhhh!" hissed Baby.

"Yes, the last one is called Zebulon. He flew me home," Kitty explained, reliving her flight home across the city's rooftops. "Zebulon told me that the bogeyman is responsible for the gargoyles disappearing. He is also to blame for the wishing well and the bad wishes. The thing is, Zebulon thought I would know how to shut down the wishing well."

"I knew this too," said Roger. "Some of us were up early this morning."

"Wait," said Baby ignoring him. "Didn't the book of magic show us a picture of a gargoyle?"

"Yes!"

"Aren't they supposed to know what to do?" grumbled Nutmeg.

"Well, they don't. I thought that at least I've found them, maybe we could all figure this out together. But then Zebulon vanished too."

"What was that about being arrested?" asked Roger.

Kitty took a deep breath. "Marcus Snodgrass snitched on me for breaking into the library. I've just been interviewed by the police and sentenced to community service with Marcus on Monday night—in the library grounds."

The cats were silent for a moment and then Roger said, "Well, it could have been worse. You haven't been kicked out, you still have a home."

"It's worse than that!"

"Worse?"

"Yes, I've been sent to my room, for the whole day."

"Oh, is that all? They'll still feed you then?"

"Well of course they'll still feed me," snapped Kitty. Roger did not understand how awful this was.

"Still got your bed and your food? All's well then! They'll forget about it in a few days, mark my words." Roger started licking his tail. As a life-long homeless cat, he considered a good meal and a warm bed about as good as it got.

"You said the library grounds?" Baby asked. "That's the old graveyard. What do they want you to do out there at night?"

"No idea," Kitty huffed.

"I don't like it, seems fishy to me," said Nutmeg.

"Well, no need to worry about the night stealers, they're out and about causing havoc. Don't reckon they'll be returning to the library any time soon," said Roger.

"And that's another problem," said Kitty. "Last night on the way to the Midsummer's Parade, we passed two houses where the police had been called about little hairy men raiding pantries, eating all the food and making a mess. Then I heard them, I mean, I heard that horrible cry they make and I know it was them. Everything is such a mess and it's all my fault."

Kitty started to cry.

Nutmeg and Roger exchanged uncomfortable glances.

Baby jumped up on the bed, gently rubbing her face against Kitty's. "It will all work out you know, it always does. We'll fix it, we'll fix it all. The night stealers, the wishing well, the bogeyman and the missing gargoyles. We'll make it all right and we'll do it together. Won't we?" She turned to face Nutmeg and Roger.

"Yes, yes, right you are, um, we will!" said Roger.

Nutmeg nodded, unconvinced.

Footsteps echoed down the stairs. The cats disappeared. By now Kitty could tell they were Grandpa's footsteps. He knocked on her bedroom door and then peeked inside. "We're going out for a walk. You will stay in your room while we're gone, won't you?"

"Yes Grandpa," said Kitty.

He closed the door and his footsteps faded away.

The cats came out from their hiding place under the bed.

"Now what?" asked Nutmeg.

"Tell them what we found out this morning." Roger nudged Kitty's leg. "We were up and at it early." He puffed out his chest.

A grin slid across Kitty's face.

"Yes, we were." Kitty reached a hand out to pet Roger's head. "We found that the secret passageways end up in Dr. McKracken's attic study."

Kitty pulled the photograph out of her pocket. "And I found this—" She held out the photograph. "Have you seen her?"

All three cats leaned in.

"Nope," said Nutmeg stretching.

"No, I'm sorry," said Baby.

"Not that I remember," Roger said. "Although she does look like the type to feed me."

"I wonder..." Kitty thought out loud. "I wonder if I could ask the book of magic, do you think it might give me an answer?"

"It's worth a try," said Baby.

Kitty pulled the book out from under her bed. It looked so ordinary and smelled like the damp crypt.

Reaching into the pocket of her hoodie, she pulled out the licorice stick. Nutmeg and Baby sat either side of her and Roger retreated under the bed while she chanted, "North, south, east, west, practical magic is the best!" Tapping the directions out on the book, she swirled her stick around like a magic wand before touching the cover.

A series of brass cogs and wheels appeared, clicking as each lock sprang free. The book sparkled and then quadrupled in size with a slight pop.

Kitty put the licorice stick in her mouth, chewing on the end before opening the book to the contents page. "I'm looking for a woman holding a baby."

The book sat motionless.

"Now what?" asked Kitty.

"Maybe you need to add something?" said Nutmeg.

"Add what?" Kitty waved the licorice stick over the book without even thinking about it.

The book jumped to one side and the contents page began

rewriting itself, getting longer and longer. Lots of sums started appearing all over the page as if scrawled by an invisible hand. Just one or two neat additions and subtractions at first but then they started to fill the margins with long division.

The contents page continued to grow. It was now so much longer than the book that it curled into a scroll on the floor.

"Maybe your question needed more, you know, ingredients," said Roger helpfully.

Cake recipes appeared.

"Don't you mean information, Roger?" asked Kitty. A cloud of white powder puffed out of the book and into her face.

Kitty licked her lips. "Sugar!"

An even bigger puff of a heavier white powder came next.

"That'll be the flour," said Roger, sticking his tongue out.

"Stop it before the recipe gets to the eggs!" cried Nutmeg in horror, diving under the bed.

"Stop!" Kitty shouted waving her wand.

The scroll rolled up, the book spun around, popped back to its normal size and with a puff of powdered sugar, the cover slammed shut.

"That was close," said Nutmeg, peering from under the bed. Baby was next to him, Roger behind in the farthest corner.

Kitty turned back to the book. "I have an idea," she said with a smile.

"Oh dear," said Nutmeg, backing further away.

Holding the photograph in front of the book, Kitty waved her licorice stick wand and said, "Show me the woman in this photograph."

The book strained like it was about to explode, groaned and then belched yellow smoke.

A door popped up out of the book. It was around three feet high and purple.

Kitty looked over at the cats. "What now?"

"We go through it," said Baby.

14 THE WITCH'S COTTAGE

"YOU GO FIRST," grumbled Nutmeg, eyeing the strange purple door with suspicion.

"Well, alright then…" Kitty took out the Timekeeper and pressed the button on the top, just in case this door took her into Fairyland or some other magical place where time worked differently. Pressing this button would keep her in real time and save her from getting stuck in Fairyland.

On her hands and knees, she crawled through the small purple door and into a cottage.

She glanced over her shoulder and saw Nutmeg and Baby both trying to squeeze through at the same time.

"I'll stay here, you know, as a lookout." Roger winked and then curled up in a ball on Kitty's bed and went straight to sleep.

Kitty rolled her eyes at Roger and turned her attention to the cottage she had just crawled into. An old woman was stirring a big black cauldron over an open fireplace. The woman was tall and thin and dressed in black from head to foot. The steam from the cauldron made her curly, gray hair stick out in all directions.

"You won't be needing your Timekeeper, this is not Fairyland," she said without turning around. "Oh, and please tell your friends to either come or go, it's drafty with that door open." Baby and Nutmeg tumbled through the door in a heap.

"Is this really your house?"

"No of course not, I lived in a room above a shop. This is the house I would love to have lived in. This is the house of my dreams." The witch stepped back from the cauldron and turned to sit in her rocking chair. She looked around wistfully before picking up her knitting. The knitting needles click-clacked and an enormous woolly thing dangled beneath them. Kitty didn't want to ask what it was.

Kitty studied her. She was definitely the woman in the photograph. Only maybe a bit younger. And taller.

"What's your name?" Kitty asked.

"Beatrice Witcher."

"You see, I have this photo and we're both in it."

"I know," said Beatrice Witcher without looking up from her knitting.

Kitty took a step closer to the woman and the floorboards creaked loudly.

The cottage had everything Kitty expected a witch's cottage to have. A broomstick and a slightly crumpled witch's hat hung on the wall by the door. The room was an odd shape with lots of nooks stuffed with books and potion bottles. A collection of cauldrons were piled up in the corner. Every size from the smallest thimble to as big as Dr. McKracken's jam making pot.

"Take a seat, dear." The knitting needles kept clicking.

The only place to sit was on an old couch in the center of the room. Kitty sat down on the baggy sofa and sank so deeply into it she was almost swallowed. Glancing around, her eyes stopped on a large cuckoo clock perched on the wall. It looked just like the one she had seen in the room of the past where she had learned the secret to unlocking the book of magic.

The book she was now inside.

Both cats were sniffing carefully around the room.

Kitty's gaze fell upon the bubbling cauldron.

"What are you making?"

"Soup."

"Magical soup?"

"No, cheese and turnip. Would you like some?"

Without waiting for a response, the witch put down her knitting, got up and unhooked a huge black ladle from the wall, filling a wooden bowl. "Here you are, dear." The witch handed her the bowl and a crust of bread. The loaf had no doubt been baked in the very same fire.

Kitty lifted the spoon to her lips and tasted the soup. It was delicious. She didn't realize how hungry she was until she started eating and was scraping the bottom of the bowl before she knew it. Both cats were already asleep by the fire. Somehow this made her feel even more at ease.

The cuckoo clock cuckooed.

"Now then, you must have questions of a profoundly magical nature, or else you wouldn't be here."

"Where is here?"

"Inside the book of course. Only a small number of my closest magical friends were instructed in the incantations necessary to open the book and reveal its true contents," Beatrice said with a flourish of her bat-winged arm.

"The book..." Kitty thought a moment. "Are you the same person as B. Witcher, the author of the book?"

"The very same! Well almost." Beatrice chose her words carefully. "I am a not a physical person. I don't have a body like you or your friends here. I exist as a memory of Beatrice Witcher." Seeing the confused look on Kitty's face Beatrice said, "I'm a magical copy. I was created to be a keeper of magical knowledge, a guardian of this book's secrets."

"How? I mean, how are we inside the book?"

"Enchantment!" Beatrice shrieked. "After the book was written, I, I mean the real Beatrice Witcher, enchanted it to become a storehouse for all of the magical knowledge she gained during her lifetime. Because such a book would be too large for anyone to read or any shelf to hold, she made it respond to questions, only bringing forth that magical information relevant to the queries posed." Beatrice smiled and bowed, as if she had just finished a theatrical performance.

"Where do you keep all the magic?"

"Follow me." She walked across the room and pulled open a narrow doorway next to the fireplace. Kitty imagined it to be a cupboard door, but when Beatrice disappeared into it, she got up and followed her.

Kitty gasped. She was standing in an enormous library. Clouds hung where there should have been a ceiling. The shelves reached up, disappearing into puffy white depths. There seemed to be no end to it.

The door shut behind her.

"Now," said Beatrice Witcher. "Let's find out a little bit more about you."

"Cor! Cor!" Something creaked and whirred overhead, circled and then landed on Beatrice's shoulder.

"Hello Munin." Beatrice stroked a crow-shaped machine on the head.

"What is that?" Kitty gasped, never having seen a mechanical bird.

"Kitty Tweddle, meet Munin, the librarian."

"Wow!"

Munin inclined his head toward Kitty. Like the inner workings of a watch, he was a collection of brass cogs and wheels with a small red alarm clock for a heart.

"Well, say hello Munin," said Beatrice.

Munin sat motionless on Beatrice's shoulder with his head bowed.

"He must need a wind-up. He's clockwork you see."

"Where do you wind him up?"

"His tail, it's a key."

Kitty ran her hands along his body, reaching his tail.

Very gently, she wound him up. Springs tightened, cogs turned and Munin sprang to life, flapping his wings and bobbing his head up and down.

Beatrice shuffled along the bookshelves muttering. She waved her hand, and the whole bookshelf started to move. This shelf contained not books, but boxes. Old, shabby cardboard ones.

"Kitty Tweddle..." She muttered as she waved her hand and the shelf whizzed by at lightning speed, revealing a new set of boxes.

Munin pecked at one of them.

Kitty walked around to stand next to Beatrice and get a better look. The boxes all had names on them, handwritten in black marker pen. Some of the boxes were tiny, some were massive.

"How strange, I don't see you. They are all kept alphabetically you see and you should be right here." She pointed a bony finger forward.

"Cor! Cor!" Munin crowed.

Kitty took a step back. "Um, I think I am there—look!"

"Oh my, it's so big I couldn't see it!"

In front of them, standing almost as high as a house was a box with Kitty Tweddle written on it in six foot high letters. Munin hopped along the top of it, pecking happily.

Beatrice looked Kitty up and down. "You must be very important to have a box this big. Let's see what's inside."

Producing a wand from up her sleeve, Beatrice waved it at the box, muttering words Kitty couldn't understand.

A small door opened at the front of the box and a red rubber hand bounced out on a spring.

Kitty leaned in to see what it was holding.

Beatrice picked up a long thin metal tube and said, "Thank you," to the hand. It disappeared back inside the box.

"What is it?"

"A Crystalizer."

"What does it do?"

"It will show us what we need to know about you."

Kitty held her breath. Would it show her breaking into the library? Or Dr. McKracken's study? Or something worse?

Holding it up to her eye like a telescope, Beatrice twisted the dial left and right. "Hmmm... Well... I see... My, my..."

Munin flew down to her shoulder and nudged her aside to take a look himself. Taking his beady eye away from the Crystalizer, he let out a sorrowful, "Cor!"

Beatrice turned to Kitty with a sad look on her face. "It would seem the real Beatrice Witcher disappeared the night you were born. This was the very last entry she made into her magical journal. Right after she bound your magical powers to hide you from *him*."

"You mean the bogeyman?"

"I'm afraid so."

"May I see?"

Beatrice handed Kitty the Crystalizer. "Just twist the dial until it comes into focus."

Holding the Crystalizer up to her eye, Kitty gazed through the eyepiece. At first she could only see vivid patterns, like a kaleidoscope. As she adjusted the dial, a scene came into focus. An old woman who looked a lot like Beatrice was standing in front of a window while lightning crackled and thunder boomed outside.

In the next scene, the old woman was sitting next to a bed, holding a baby.

"That's my mum!" Kitty cried out, recognizing the woman in the bed. "She looks so young. That baby must be me."

The scene changed, and now the old woman was spinning blue light from the ends of her fingers and wrapping it around the baby like a cocoon.

The last scene showed Kitty's mum promising to bring Kitty back for magical training before her twelfth birthday, when the magical bindings blocking her powers and shielding her from the bogeyman, wore off.

Kitty handed the Crystalizer back to Beatrice, not sure what to make of it all.

Sighing deeply, Beatrice knocked on the box. The red hand sprang out and she handed it the Crystalizer.

"Munin and I will help you in any way we can," she said softly, placing a hand on Kitty's shoulder. Then, she waved the bookshelf holding Kitty's enormous box away and marched back in the direction of the door.

Munin left them and flew away into the library.

Following Beatrice back into the cottage, Kitty flopped down on the couch without a word.

Sitting in her rocking chair, Beatrice pinched her lips into a thin line, her eyebrows knitted into one dark furrow across her forehead. "Now, tell me the exact nature of your most pressing magical question."

Kitty took a deep breath. "Well, I need to shut down a wishing well. And I want to know why everyone one was staring at me on Midsummer's Eve, and I'm a bit worried about doing community service at the library at night and—"

"My goodness!" Beatrice held up her hands. "That's a lot. Perhaps we need to start with the first one, the wishing well..." Her eyes moved up and to one side as if she was remembering something. "You have asked the book about the wishing well before and I believe you were given an answer."

"Yes, a picture actually, of a gargoyle."

"The book always offers the most concise answer possible." Beatrice beamed. "But be warned... The book answers the question asked, not what you thought you meant, or what you really need to know." She raised an eyebrow.

Kitty thought about this for a moment. "I found the gargoyles and they didn't know what to do, other than sing."

"Ah, the beauty of gargoyle-song! Perhaps sing is all they need do. Never underestimate the power of music, it can shuffle the stars in the heavens."

Nutmeg was snoring by the fire. Beatrice reached for a poker and stoked the coals. "As to your question about the strange people on Midsummer's Eve..." The embers glowed orange like an erupting volcano and sparks flew up the chimney.

Beatrice stared into the flames before continuing. "When a person has magical powers, all others who are magical in nature can sense it. Magic is like a light that shines from the core of your being. That's what happened to you on Midsummer's Eve, the others staring at you were magical beings themselves. Couldn't you sense their magic?"

Kitty shook her head. She hadn't sensed anything. It was a weird night all in all. The Snodgrasses had joined them— which ruined it right away. Emily had stolen the Timekeeper, Marcus had tried to take her money and then she had gotten lost and chased through the catacombs beneath the city by a masked birdman and his mob. No, she hadn't sensed any magic. She had been too busy trying to escape.

"Not to worry, perhaps it will come... in time," Beatrice reassured her, poking the fire again. "However, time is something we do not have." She turned to stare at Kitty and squinted.

Kitty felt the weight of that stare but said nothing.

The fire crackled.

"Beatrice Witcher, the writer of this book, whose magical memories I hold, made your mother promise to send you here for training before your bindings unwrapped on your twelfth birthday. I believe that Munin and I must step in and do whatever we can to train you in their use."

"So... What's first?"

"You must arm yourself Kitty Tweddle, for I suspect the forces of evil are vast and growing in number and you must be ready when they descend upon you like a plague of summer frogs after a long drought!" Beatrice said. "It is very dangerous for a magical person to go around unguarded. It's like walking around with the Crown Jewels on. It will attract a lot of unwanted attention. You must learn to shield yourself, swathe yourself in a veil of magic." She waved her arms around. "I can teach you how. I call it, The Mantle."

Kitty sat up. This was real magic and she was ready to

learn. "Will this mean I won't be followed by the birdman or his mob anymore?"

"Yes."

"Or the bogeyman?"

"Certainly."

Kitty smiled.

"All magic begins with a thought. Imagination is the most powerful magic you possess." Beatrice stood in front of the fireplace, the orange flames casting an eerie glow behind her. She stooped lower until she was almost nose to nose with Kitty. "Now, let's take a look inside your mind and see what kind of imagination you possess."

Kitty's eyes went wide.

Beatrice rose back up to her full height. "I will give you a word or phrase, you must immediately describe it. Use all of your senses, give me a color, a texture, a smell, a sound, a size, give me..." her voice dropped to a whisper making Kitty lean in. "Give me a feeling!"

Beatrice paused for effect before booming, "Elephant!"

"Big, gray, smelly, floppy ears, rough skin, um... sharp tusks..." Kitty spluttered.

"Kippers!"

"Stinky, fishing boat, the sea, fins, salty, and um..." Kitty stammered. "Hooks, nets, fishermen..."

"The forest!"

"Green, wood, trees, rivers, bumble bees, leaves, stingy nettles... eh, smells like dirt and grass... um..."

"How do you *feel* in the forest?"

"Watched."

"Good. Now we're getting somewhere." Beatrice nodded and then her eyes narrowed. "Watched by?"

"The animals, the trees, the air, the forest itself..." Kitty trailed off. She wasn't sure where the words were coming from or if she believed them.

Beatrice smiled and folded her arms. "Excellent."

"How does this help me shield myself?"

"Mist!"

"Swirling, can't see, no smell, surrounding... lost..."

"You have just imagined The Mantle. You must shield yourself with The Mantle so that you cannot be seen or smelled, or felt. You will disappear like mist to those who attempt to pursue you." Beatrice put her hands on her hips and looked very satisfied with herself.

"Pay attention, this is how it is done." Beatrice closed her eyes. "Bring to mind the mist, see it, feel it, imagine it surrounding you..."

A mistiness came from out of nowhere and filled the room, making everything foggy until Kitty couldn't see a thing.

"Now, become the mist."

The misty room cleared, but Beatrice Witcher was gone.

"Ms. Witcher? Are you still here?" Kitty stood up and turned around, looking for her.

"Yes, I am right in front of you, I have not moved."

Kitty stared straight ahead and into the fireplace. If Beatrice Witcher was in front of her, then she was quite invisible. "Can I do this?"

"Yes, you can." Beatrice shimmered back into view. "Now you try. Head up, shoulders back, deep breath and..." She raised her eyebrows expectantly.

Kitty stood up straight, took a breath, closed her eyes and imagined the mist, how it looked, felt and smelled. A cloud formed in the middle of the room, hovered for a moment and then disappeared.

"Not bad, take a *deep* breath and try again."

Kitty closed her eyes and breathed deeply, calling to mind the swirl of mist, she let it writhe and twirl around. Her feet felt cold. She opened her eyes and looked down, she was standing in a puddle.

"Never mind." Beatrice waved her hand and the puddle vanished. "Try remembering a time when you were in the fog, can you recall a foggy day?"

"Yes, in the garden at number five Crescent Avenue, not long after I arrived for the summer. The garden was so misty I couldn't make out the wall at the end."

"Good, very good. Now, close your eyes, take a deep breath and bring that scene to mind."

Kitty did so and a pale mist filled the room.

"Good, good!" Beatrice waved her hand through the mist. "Now, instead of looking at the mist, imagine you *are* the mist, become it!"

Kitty imagined that she was the mist, the room began to clear and Kitty became translucent but remained a foggy version of herself.

"Now," Beatrice whispered, "let the mist disappear."

Kitty imagined herself as the mist simply vanishing. She opened her eyes and looked down at her hands, they were gone, her whole body was gone. "I did it! I disappeared!"

"No, you have not disappeared, you are wearing The Mantle and veiling your presence, you are still here." Beatrice took a step forward and placed a firm hand on Kitty's shoulder.

"Never underestimate the power of illusion, it can move worlds."

"How do I take it off?"

"That's much easier, just imagine being seen."

Kitty did her best to imagine being seen, but that didn't work and she began to panic. Then, she imagined seeing her reflection in the mirror and in an instant, she was visible. She looked down at her body, turning her hands over in wonder. A big smile spread across her face. "I'm back! I did it! I really did it!"

"Excellent, you have mastered the first skill, that of making yourself disappear. However," Beatrice said, holding up a bony finger. "You don't want to disappear completely, although it may be useful in some, rather more clandestine circumstances, complete disappearance may bring you even more unwanted attention. What you must do is shield only your magical powers, make them appear to disappear."

Kitty eyebrows knitted together. "Make my magic appear to disappear?"

"Yes, instead of putting The Mantle around your body, wrap it around your magic."

"Ah." Kitty imagined the magic inside of her to be a ball of sparkling stars. She wrapped her magic in the mist, making it disappear. "Well? Did I do it?"

Beatrice stood back and beamed at her student. "You certainly have. Now you know how to do it, wear The Mantle whenever you need to hide your magical presence. No more being chased through the streets by undesirable magical people!"

"Another matter we must discuss. I assume you have been properly instructed in the use that thing?" She nodded at the Timekeeper hanging around Kitty's neck.

Kitty nodded.

"Tell me, how far into Fairyland did you get?"

"Oh, I got in alright, I know how to use the sundial and open the doors to the future room and the past room. I've used the Seeingscope in the future room and the waterfall in the room of the past."

The old witch let out a mighty cackle. "I assume you met a helpful old woman at a spinning wheel?"

"Yes, the old hag, she showed me how to use the Seeingscope..." Kitty trailed off, unsure of herself when Beatrice grinned like she had swallowed a banana sideways. "I mean, she was helpful," Kitty stammered.

"I'll bet she was!" Beatrice raised her eyebrows. "But know this Kitty Tweddle, that old hag is nothing but a gatekeeper, and the garden with the rooms to the future and that past is nothing but a gatehouse. A distraction. Illusion doesn't just move worlds, it can conceal them. The old hag's job is to keep you there and not let you get any further."

"You mean there's more?"

"More! Oh!" Beatrice laughed so hard her whole body shook. When she finally stopped shuddering, she said, "Fairyland, the real Fairyland, lies beyond the gatehouse. Fairyland is a whole world filled with magic and monsters. And worse."

"What do you mean? What could be worse than monsters?"

The old witch sighed. "I hope you never find out."

Their heads spun around at the sound of scratching at the front door. Baby and Nutmeg were on their paws in seconds. Nutmeg reached the door first, stood up on his hind paws and released the latch. The door swung inward.

"Someone's coming!" Roger said from the other side.

"Come back soon! Always a pleasure!" Beatrice called out to Kitty's retreating form. Kitty offered her a quick smile from over her shoulder before she dived through the purple door after the cats.

Once they were all back in Kitty's bedroom, the doorway popped back into the book which quivered back to its original size. Kitty just had time to push it under her bed where all three cats were hiding, when her Grandpa knocked on the bedroom door and opened it.

"Hungry?" he said walking into the room with a tray. "I brought you a snack." He set the tray down on the desk. It smelled like soup.

Kitty didn't have the heart to say she had already eaten. "Yes please, Grandpa."

15 THE GRAVEYARD

MRS. SNODGRASS walked into her kitchen and screamed.

For the last hour, she had stood at Judith's garden gate across the street, lecturing her about the importance of cleanliness. Mrs. Snodgrass spent hours ensuring that her home, particularly the kitchen, was held to the highest standards and had insisted that Judith come along and see for herself.

The sight before her left Mrs. Snodgrass speechless. Someone had thrown flour all over the floor, along with everything inside the fridge. Open jars of peanut butter, blackcurrant jam and marmalade lay scattered, their contents smeared together as if someone had rolled in it.

From behind her, Mrs. Snodgrass heard Judith fail to stifle a giggle, her green tweed suit about to pop a button.

A loud thumping noise sounded upstairs.

Trying to regain her composure, Mrs. Snodgrass turned to Judith and said, "Can you check on that noise?"

Trying not to laugh Judith said, "Oh, yes, I'll just go and see what that is." And then she scuttled out of the kitchen.

With her mouth gaping, Mrs. Snodgrass took a step forward.

Splattered across the white tiled walls was a mural in food, finger painted by artists unknown. A mixture of ketchup, mustard, mint sauce and meatball lasagna dribbled like a setting sun onto the kitchen countertops.

Something dripped onto her nose. Mrs. Snodgrass looked up and saw that the entire ceiling was coated in strawberry pudding.

It continued to rain pudding in her kitchen when Mrs. Snodgrass screamed again, staggered backward and fell into the open fridge. A little hairy man, covered in chocolate spread and strawberry pudding giggled with delight as he ran toward her, slamming the fridge door, shutting a hysterical Mrs. Snodgrass inside.

The night stealer fell on the floor with laughter and went back to what he had been doing before she arrived—making food angels. He lay on his back, waving his arms up and down, smearing the spreads and jams into an angelic mess. He stopped now and again, opening his mouth to catch drops of strawberry pudding as they fell from the ceiling.

Judith crept upstairs. "Marcus? Emily? Is that you making all that noise?"

Someone was going through Mrs. Snodgrass's wardrobe. A night stealer fell over the hem of his dress when he stepped through the door. The dress was too long for him, despite the high heels he was wearing. The other night stealers screeched with laughter. One had found a makeup bag and put lipstick on himself, the other night stealers, the vanity mirror and all along the walls of Mrs. Snodgrass's bedroom.

In Emily's bedroom, a night stealer wearing her pink

nightdress had pulled the heads off all of her dollies and chewed the horn from her favorite fluffy pink unicorn.

Next door in Marcus's room, an electric train careered toward a night stealer who was tied to the tracks, laughing his head off as the train screamed nearer. Action men lay dismembered on the pale blue carpet, their heads and limbs scattered around the room. The whole house smelled like dog food and looked like a rubbish heap.

Judith knocked politely on Emily's bedroom door. "Hello?" She walked in.

Moments later she was chased from the house and pelted with doll heads by a night stealer wearing Mrs. Snodgrass's clothes and makeup.

Kitty's breath steamed up the bedroom window. It was the day of her community service at the library and it was raining, again. She looked out onto a haze of drizzle that lay over the garden. The miserable weather matched her mood.

She turned around to see Nutmeg twitching in his sleep at the bottom of her bed. Baby sat on top of her desk and licked a paw, washing her face. Both cats had arrived right after breakfast and promised Roger would be following soon after.

Grandpa's footsteps clumped down the stairs to the basement. Kitty listened and heard the sound of a padlock click open. He must be opening the red door at the very back of the basement. The room Kitty was forbidden to enter.

"What in the world!" Grandpa gasped when he opened the door. "Well of all the... I've seen some things in my time but never..."

Hearing him, Kitty scrambled to her feet and ran out of her room. "What is it, Grandpa?" she called down the corridor.

Grandpa was leaning against the door frame, wiping his brow with a handkerchief. "What's this?" He leaned down and stretched out his hand.

Kitty saw what Grandpa was reaching for. A shiny penny. "No!"

Too late.

He picked it up.

His body stiffened, his clothes got baggy, but he didn't shrink. In fact, his head began to swell and turned bright orange.

Kitty reached him in time to see his face transform into a pumpkin head, carved with a jagged grin. Straw sprouted from the cuffs of his shirt and trousers, spilling from beneath a hat on his pumpkin head.

The bad penny had turned Grandpa into a scarecrow. He leaned up against the door, frozen stiff.

Leaning away in shock, Kitty's back pushed against the unlocked door to the forbidden room. It creaked open and she peered over her shoulder, her eyes widening at what she saw inside. Now she knew what had surprised her Grandpa so much when he unlocked the door.

Last time she had peeked into this room was the night she arrived. It had poured with rain and all Kitty saw in her brief glimpse was a puddle on the floor.

But now the room, once dark and dingy, was filled with glowing light. It danced about like smoke on water. In the middle of the room stood a wishing well. It had a round base and a small tiled roof painted red. It was about Kitty's height and made of wood. The only things that seemed to be missing were a bucket and a handle.

Kitty gaped at the wishing well like a fish.

She remembered her conversation with Grandpa on

Midsummer's Eve as they walked to the carnival. He had told her about a friend, Beatrice, who claimed that the old Penny Well was buried under the floor. That must have been the puddle she saw, water rising from the old well due to the heavy rains. Beatrice had also told him the well was filled with wild magic. Enough to make a wishing well appear?

Suddenly, someone hammered on the front door upstairs, snapping Kitty out of her thoughts.

"Help! Help!" A woman's voice shrieked through the letterbox.

Kitty heard Grandma's footsteps cross the floor above.

Leaving her Grandpa propped up near the door to the forbidden room, Kitty ran back to her bedroom. Ripping the tapestry from the wall, she pulled open the door to the secret passageways, flipped on her keyring flashlight and bounded up the stairs. Familiar with the narrow path, she made it quickly up to the top, tumbling through the tiny door into Dr. McKracken's attic study.

Striding across the floor, she frantically searched the bottles and jars on the shelves, looking for one in particular. A small vial filled with dark purple liquid and a black stopper.

Swirling movement caught her eye. Her gaze locked on the bottle labeled *antidote to wishes*. She grabbed it, stuffed it into her pocket and was bounding back down the stairs within a flash.

Reaching her Grandpa, she pulled the tiny vial from her pocket. When Dr. McKracken had used it on her, he dabbed a little on a boil on the end of her nose. There was nothing to dab on Grandpa. He had been completely transformed into a scarecrow.

Kitty unstoppered the cork and magic flared from her fingertips. Not the wild, uncontrolled lightning sparks she experienced when running from the mob on her birthday. This time, it was a gentle, blue light that sparkled where her fingers clasped the vial.

The liquid in the bottle squirmed out of the opening and took on a misty appearance.

Kitty stared at it. Using her imagination like Beatrice Witcher had taught her, she formed a picture in her mind of how Grandpa should look. "Undo this wicked wish," she commanded and held the vial up to the pumpkin's nose.

Purple smoke streamed from the vial seeping up the pumpkin head's carved nostrils. The pumpkin bubbled, then quivered.

Kitty held her breath.

The pumpkin head crumpled in on itself and then rippled away revealing Grandpa's face. The straw sprouting from his cuffs vanished and his clothes shivered as they returned to normal.

"Good g-grief!" Grandpa stammered and clutched the doorframe for support.

Kitty stuffed the empty vial back in her pocket.

"Grandpa, are you alright?"

"Yes, yes, I'm fine." Pulling a handkerchief out of his pocket, he mopped his brow. "Not sure what happened there." He stood up straight, appearing restored.

Now that Grandpa was back to himself, Kitty became aware of a commotion upstairs. Someone was sobbing.

Grandpa heard it too and turned to climb the stairs.

Kitty pulled the door to the forbidden room closed and ran up the stairs behind Grandpa to find a bedraggled Mrs. Snodgrass on all fours in the upstairs hallway.

Grandma was kneeling on the floor, consoling Mrs. Snodgrass. She looked up at their approach and shrugged.

"They licked chocolate spread from the jar, from the jar!" Mrs. Snodgrass screeched. Something pink and gooey dripped from her hair onto the rug. Her face was covered in flour. "They locked me in the fridge! My kitchen, my beautiful clean kitchen, smeared in jam…" She began to cry.

Kitty didn't think Mrs. Snodgrass was capable of crying.

"Who did this?" Grandpa kneeled down on the rug next to Mrs. Snodgrass and tried to comfort her.

"Little… hairy… men," she sniffed between sobs. "Bathing in pudding and finger-painting food all over the walls." Mrs. Snodgrass collapsed into a blubbering wreck.

"There, there dear." Grandpa patted her shoulder lightly and looked hopelessly from Kitty to Grandma.

The clock made a clicking sound. *Bong! Bong! Bong! Bong! Bong! Bong! Bong!*

"I'm supposed to be at the library," said Kitty. "With Marcus."

"Mrs. Snodgrass?" Grandpa said. "Where is Marcus?"

Mrs. Snodgrass's head snapped up. "Marcus, my son!" She leaped up and bolted out of the door.

Kitty looked at her Grandpa, he shook his head.

Tearing along the garden path, Mrs. Snodgrass reached the garden gate just as Marcus was rounding the street corner. "Marcus! Marcus!"

Marcus reached his mother at the gate of number five. "Mother, what have you done to yourself?" He leaned away from her when she reached out to him.

Mrs. Snodgrass's tears streaked through the flour, mixing with pink pudding on her face. It made her look like a scary Halloween clown.

"Where is Emily?" she whimpered.

"At violin practice, where she is every Monday evening."

Grandpa reached the gate. "Why don't you go inside Mrs. Snodgrass?"

"Yes, I'll make you a cup of tea," said Grandma.

"And then I'll take these two to the library for their community service. When I get back, we'll sort this business out," Grandpa said.

"No, no, you mustn't leave me." Mrs. Snodgrass clung to Grandpa's arm. "I'm coming with you."

"All right dear," Grandpa said, patting her hand. "We'll all go together."

Marcus got on the other side of Grandpa, wanting to be as far away from his pudding covered mother as possible, leaving Kitty to walk beside Mrs. Snodgrass, who reached out and held her hand so tightly Kitty thought it might fall off.

Mr. Wolf looked at his watch as they approached. "Good evening," he said and smiled a crooked smile. "I was wondering if you had decided not to bother and run off," he said with a chuckle.

No one else laughed.

His brow creased. "My dear Mrs. Snodgrass, what on earth has happened to you?"

Mrs. Snodgrass just shook her pudding-encrusted head before burying it into Grandpa's shoulder, sobbing silently.

"Good gracious, what is going on?" asked Mr. Wolf.

"Nothing to worry about I assure you, Mr. Wolf," Grandpa said casually. "I'm taking Mrs. Snodgrass home right now as a matter of fact. I assume we can entrust Kitty and Marcus to your care for the length of their community service?" Grandpa nodded and took a step backward, taking Mrs. Snodgrass with him.

"Certainly Mr. Tweddle, of course. The children will be perfectly safe with me." He clasped his hands together.

Marcus gave Kitty a quick dig in the ribs. "This is all your fault," he said under his breath.

Kitty rolled her eyes.

Mr. Wolf stood with his hands on his hips. "Right then, got some work for the two of you this evening in the graveyard."

"What!" Marcus's face was pink with frustration. "We're supposed to be doing stuff in the library, not the graveyard!"

"I am sure you are aware that the library sits on the foundations of the old chapel, and therefore the old chapel grounds *are* the library grounds." Mr. Wolf glared. "You *are* doing stuff in the library, Marcus."

Kitty remained silent, not wanting to make things any worse. She knew that Mr. Wolf would pick some horrible job for them to do. It was punishment after all. She was just glad they weren't down in that creepy crypt. She looked down at her shoes, waiting to hear exactly what that punishment was.

"You'll need these." Mr. Wolf handed them each a butter knife.

Kitty and Marcus glanced at each other and then at the butter knives.

"Follow me." Mr. Wolf picked up a bag and strode ahead into the old graveyard. Neither of them had a chance to ask what the knives were for.

Although it was still light, the shadows were starting to lengthen and the sky grew dim. The headstones, which were hundreds of years old, stuck out in all directions. Some leaned forward, others leaned back, some propped each other up. One or two had fallen over completely and grass grew up around them.

The furthest part of the graveyard was the grandest, with the largest headstones and even some big boxy tombs. A life-sized stone angel with a veiled head sat reading a book. Another angel sculpture was slumped over a grave, weeping.

There was another tomb further back, under the branches of an overgrown yew tree. It was dark under the tree and Kitty couldn't quite make it all out.

Mr. Wolf turned left and stopped next to some enormous gravestones. "This is as far as we need to go." He waited for Kitty and Marcus to catch up. "As you can see, someone has vandalized these graves." His hand swept across a small area between the ancient headstones.

There were beer bottles, paper wrappers, and other rubbish. Mr. Wolf reached into the bag he had brought with them, pulled out two battery operated lanterns and lit them, placing one either side of the graves. He then handed Kitty and Marcus each a plastic bag.

"What's this for?" Marcus asked.

"Picking up the rubbish."

"What about the butter knives?" Kitty asked.

"Ah, yes, see here?" Mr. Wolf pointed to a pink splodge on the side of a gravestone. "Bubblegum. Use the butter knife to pick it off."

"Ugh! That's been in someone's mouth," said Marcus.

"And it's going to go in that rubbish bag you're holding," said Mr. Wolf.

Kitty sighed, *the sooner we get this over with the better.*

"I'll leave you to get on with it and check back in an hour or so. I have another job for you after you're finished here." He strode off toward the library without another word.

"Unbelievable!" Marcus threw his bag on the ground and flopped down. "I can't believe we have to do this."

"Well if you'd just kept your mouth shut, we wouldn't be here," said Kitty.

Marcus glared and his face went purple.

Kitty picked up his rubbish bag and handed it to him. "The sooner we get this done, the sooner we can go home." She turned around and glanced at the library. It looked deserted. Dusk was settling in all around them and yet there were no lights on in the library. Surely Mr. Wolf was there— where else would he be?

"This is useless," said Marcus.

"Do your best. Anyway, it's getting dark and I don't want to be sitting in a graveyard at night." Kitty looked around.

Picking up the rubbish was easy. Picking the bubblegum off the gravestones with a butter knife was harder. It had been a warm day and the gum was sticky, gluing the knife to the gravestone in a pink mess.

The shadows grew longer as the sun dipped below the treetops, turning the clouds orange. The light from the lanterns attracted insects that buzzed between them.

"My lantern is going out." Marcus said, shaking it. The lantern flickered and dimmed.

"Here," said Kitty reaching into her pocket and pulling out the little LED flashlight her Grandpa had given her. "Use this." She handed it to him.

A rustling sound by the yew tree made their heads snap around. It was completely dark under the tree. Kitty squinted trying to see what had made the noise when it happened again.

Marcus held up the tiny flashlight. "What is it?"

"I don't know."

The lower branches moved. Kitty's heart beat picked up, something was prowling around.

Red eyes like hot coals peered from the shadows and a hulking shaggy dog came into view.

Kitty froze. The red eyes stared straight at her.

Not at Marcus, at her.

Too late, Kitty remembered The Mantle. With all the commotion at the house, she had forgotten to weave the spell and shield her magic. This thing must be a magical being and she was all alone and unprotected in a graveyard at dusk.

Standing tall, Kitty closed her eyes and imagined a rolling mist surrounding her. The red eyes shifted, searching for her, unable to see her magic anymore, it grunted and then withdrew deeper into the shadows.

"What *are* you doing?" asked Marcus.

"Nothing."

"How are we getting along?"

Marcus and Kitty jumped. Mr. Wolf appeared right behind them. Smiling he said, "I think that's enough out here for now, grab your stuff and come inside, I've got another job for you."

Marcus and Kitty did as they were told. Gathering up their rubbish bags, they followed Mr. Wolf back in the direction of the library.

"Shouldn't we turn the lights on?" asked Kitty when they reached the steps leading up to the library back door.

"There's no need, there are no lights where we're going," said Mr. Wolf.

Chills ran down Kitty's spine. She could think of only one place in the library where there were no electric lights.

The crypt.

16 THE HEART STONE

KITTY REMEMBERED the last time she went down the old stone steps into the crypt. How scared the cats had been, the dripping water, the slimy walls, the open coffins and the skeletons with their sightless eyes. And of course, the musty old books crawling with spiders. She did not want to go there again.

As they approached the secret entrance to the crypt, Kitty noticed that the table and chairs that usually sat in front of the doorway had been moved.

With a flick of his hand, Mr. Wolf activated the secret panel. It swung open on silent hinges. "After you," he said to Kitty.

"Why are we going down here?" Her tummy had gone all wobbly, the way it did when she was about to do something she thought she shouldn't. She had a really bad feeling about this.

"Some old books need to be sorted out," Mr. Wolf said curtly. "Come along now, the sooner we get finished the better. You have the lamp—lead on!"

Kitty walked through the secret door and began descending the steps into the crypt. She felt sick. The crypt looked exactly the way she had left it. The bookcase she had knocked over was still there and books were scattered everywhere. The slime still oozed in the corner of the room and all the skeletons remained hidden within their stone coffins, or so she hoped.

Holding up the lantern, her feet crunched down the steps. Glancing down, her eyes widened in horror.

The stairs were littered with tiny bones.

Then she realized that hers were the only footsteps she could hear. The others were not following.

She looked around at Marcus. He had gone strangely silent. He appeared stunned, his eyes as wide as saucers, his mouth frozen in a silent *no!*

Her lantern flickered and started to dim. It had been on for hours, the battery must be running out.

Mr. Wolf stood at the top of the stairs with his hand grasping Marcus's shoulder.

"I'm afraid this is where we leave you," said Mr. Wolf.

"Wha... what do you mean?" Kitty stammered, fear getting the better of her.

"I mean, I am leaving you down there, and we are going to lock this door, and walk away."

Kitty's eyes went wide as the realization of what was happening set in.

"You're going to lock me in the crypt, alone? Why?"

"I no longer need you."

"What did you ever need me for?"

"Your magical power of course! It's been leaching out of you since you arrived, fuelling my great work!"

What work was he talking about? And how could she have been so wrong about him? He seemed so... so nice.

"Someone will find me! I'll scream and scream until someone hears me!" she blurted out, panic shooting through her body.

"The library will be closed for the rest of the week, due to some reason I'll make up. No one will come anywhere near here in days. And by the time they do, well, you will have joined our skeletal friends here." He waved his arm around toward the stone coffins.

"Marcus will tell someone, won't you Marcus?"

Marcus stood as still as a statue, frozen with fear.

"No, Marcus will not. I am taking Marcus and his family back into Fairyland. But of course, you know about Fairyland don't you, Kitty? I will leave them there and return with three of my associates. Then, we will go back and invite your grandparents and Dr. McKracken to join the Snodgrasses, exchanging them for more of my kind."

Kitty gasped, realizing who he really was.

"You!" she hissed. "All this time... you're the bogeyman!"

Mr. Wolf chuckled.

"You'll never get my grandparents to go with you." Kitty pressed him.

"I assure you, my associates can be most persuasive. They will go, and never return. Meanwhile you, Kitty Tweddle, will become a permanent part of this crypt."

He moved back to the doorway, pulling Marcus with him. "Goodbye, Kitty Tweddle." He turned and disappeared. The door shut, locking with a click behind him.

Kitty raced up the steps after them, sending little crunchy bones flying everywhere. Her lantern dimmed with each passing second. She threw herself at the door, hoping it would swivel around again.

It did not.

She reasoned that because it turned on a central hinge, all she needed to do was push the opposite side and it should swing open, but it didn't work. She realized with a sinking heart, that the door could only be opened from the other side.

There has to be a way out. There has to be! Her mind raced.

With the last weak glimmer of light from her lamp, Kitty dashed back down the stairs, searching for another door she may have missed. She went straight to the back of the crypt where it was darkest, where the night stealers had been nesting before she had awoken them. It was very smelly and her feet crunched over more bones.

The lamp started to flicker. She cast it quickly about the wall, its fading light revealing nothing but solid rock. The light flickered again, and this time went out for good, plunging her into darkness.

Kitty froze.

Her breath rasped in her throat. Her pulse pounded in her head, loud enough to deafen her. She had never felt more scared.

Thrusting her hand into her pocket, she felt around for her little LED flashlight. Only when she found nothing, did she remember giving it to Marcus in the graveyard.

Instinctively, she put her hand over her heart. That's when she felt the Timekeeper, hanging on its chain around her neck. Her hands shook as she pulled it out from under her top. Although she knew it must be dangling in her out-stretched hand, she couldn't see anything in the dark.

Perhaps the Revealer will show me a way out... Pulling it from around her neck, Kitty opened the Revealer lens on the Timekeeper and took a step forward.

She tripped over something on the floor and landed on

her belly, the breath knocked out of her. The Timekeeper jolted out of her hand, its metal tinkling when it landed in the darkness.

"No!" A sob escaped her lips and Kitty curled up into a ball on the floor of the crypt. Mr. Wolf was going to kidnap her grandparents and the Snodgrass family and there was nothing she could do to help them—or herself.

She lay whimpering on the floor, tears ran down her cheeks and her body shuddered.

Then a red flicker caught her eye.

Drawing herself to her knees, Kitty gasped as tiny red fireflies appeared in front of her, more and more of them spilling from a dark object on the floor.

With the light from the fireflies, Kitty could see the Timekeeper. Only the back had popped open when she dropped it and something had fallen out. She remembered what Dr. McKracken had said about the Heart Stone, the red stone fitted into the back of the Timekeeper.

The Heart Stone will always lead back home, no matter how far its bearer wanders.

As more fireflies poured out, a red glow shone out from the exposed Heart Stone. Kitty held it up. Although it was not as bright as the lamp, it was enough to see the crypt clearly. She picked up the Timekeeper and popped the Heart Stone back inside.

The fireflies seemed to gather in certain places, burning red like the Heart Stone before drifting on, searching the chamber.

Kitty watched them fly around the walls, sparkles of ruby light moving around old books, through spiders webs and probing the skulls in their coffins, glinting from their empty eye sockets.

The fireflies did not linger around the bones but moved on, carefully and meticulously searching, like glittery red fingers prying into every crevice.

Kitty held her breath and watched them hover. They gathered against the wall covered in slime. Kitty waited, but the fireflies did not move. She walked up to the wall and touched it, gasping when her hand passed right through.

What looked like stone was, in fact, an old piece of cloth that had been draped in front of a hole in the wall. Through age, dirt and dripping slime, it looked just like the surrounding rock.

Searching for the edges of the cloth, she lifted it, revealing a long passageway beyond. The fireflies immediately seeped through, lingered and then reached forward, illuminating a set of narrow stone stairs with their rosy glow. She followed them as they wound up the dirt-covered steps. It was not far to go until she met with a dead end.

She wondered if it was a trapdoor above. Hear heart sank, if it was a trap door and she was still under the library, carpet may have been laid over the top. How would she get out?

The fireflies gathered around, seeming to urge her on. Kitty closed the Timekeeper while the fireflies swirled overhead. Reaching up, she pushed as hard as she could. Nothing moved. Still the fireflies danced urgently above her. She searched for a latch or handle she might have missed.

There was none.

Kitty gathered all her strength. *I'm getting out of here now!* She pushed as hard as she could and above her, stone grated on stone, just an inch, but it shifted.

"Help! Help! Can anyone hear me?" she called out.

She heard muffled voices above.

The stone above her started to move.

The fireflies flew out.

Dust fell from the opening and suddenly the trapdoor sprung free. Kitty closed her eyes, blinded by the flash of a lantern above her. Squinting, she could just make out Nutmeg's face scowling down at her.

"Well, are you coming out?" he said.

She smiled from ear to ear at the sight of Baby and Roger peering down at her. A strong if not small pair of arms reached down to help her. Holly the hunky punk pulled Kitty up.

Kitty popped her head up and looked around. It took only a moment for her to realize that she had not emerged under the library. She had not come through a trap door at all, but through a boxy looking grave in the graveyard.

"How did you find me?" Kitty asked.

"You were making such a racket, and we have very sensitive ears," said Roger.

"What happened, why were you down in the crypt alone?" asked Baby.

"Mr. Wolf locked me in!"

"Knew it," said Nutmeg.

. "No you didn't," growled Roger.

"Look, the important thing is, he's the bogeyman," Kitty said as she helped Holly heave the stone grave cover back in place.

Holly held up the lantern so that Kitty could read the words on the gravestone.

"What does it say?" asked Baby.

"In loving memory of Beatrice Witcher. Disappeared in the early hours of Midsummer's Day," Kitty read aloud.

"Disappeared? Well that explains why there is no body in this grave," said Baby.

"Or why it's not a grave at all," said Nutmeg.

"It looks like she disappeared on the day I was born too." Kitty pulled the photograph she had found in Dr. McKracken's study out from her pocket. "Right after this was taken."

"What does it all mean?" asked Baby.

"It means we need to get out of here and now," said Roger. He sniffed the air, the hairs on his back stood on end and his tail splayed out like a duster. "Trouble."

"No argument from me," said Nutmeg.

They raced out of the graveyard and got as far as the library car park when something big and dark appeared in front of them, blocking their path. Something with huge fangs and eyes of fire. Its hulking form stalked toward them. A dead rabbit hung limp in its jaws.

Kitty gasped in horror.

She knew it was the same beast she had seen prowling in the graveyard earlier. Her fingertips tingled and her instincts told it was not a dog or even a wolf, but a shapeshifter. Someone who could turn from human into bogeyman, or in this case, a bogeybeast. A creature from Fairyland.

The beast dropped the dead rabbit and turned to face Kitty. Blood dripped from its huge teeth.

"Going somewhere?" the beast growled in an all too familiar voice. A voice she had last heard in the crypt.

Kitty pulled herself up to her full height and took a deep breath, just like Beatrice Witcher had taught her.

"That's disgusting... Mr. Wolf."

All three cats crouched, ears back, fangs bared, hissing and spitting. Holly stood shaking by Kitty's side.

"Aww, five on one, hardly a fair fight," hissed Roger. "But I'll take those odds."

"Not so fast, my feral friend," Mr. Wolf growled in his bogeybeast form.

The air shimmered to either side of him and three wobbly shadows appeared. As they took shape, Kitty grimaced at the ugly trolls in front of her.

Lumbering gray hulks with vacant eyes and pot bellies. One of them had boogers hanging out of his nostrils.

Kitty's nose wrinkled. The trolls stunk.

"Well, well, you escaped the crypt in record time. Bravo," Mr. Wolf sneered.

"You left me to die down there!"

"Oh Kitty, I had faith in your abilities. Consider it more of a test. And I must say, you have surpassed my highest expectations. I'm proud of you," Mr. Wolf mocked.

The angrier Kitty got, the more she could feel the magic surging through her body, shooting down through her palms.

I must control it!

Looking at his troll henchmen, the bogeyman continued, "But now I am afraid I must—"

The wing mirror of a nearby car shattered. Kitty and the cats ducked as glass and plastic flew everywhere.

"Did you do that?" Roger said out of the side of his mouth.

"I didn't mean to, but I think so," said Kitty.

"Impressive." Roger grinned.

"Get them!" the bogeyman roared.

The trolls lumbered forward, thick arms outstretched. One of them stepped over a drain cover.

Kitty held out her hands in self defense. Water shot up from the drain, blasting the troll into the air.

Using the distraction, Nutmeg pounced to the side of the bogeybeast, nipping at its heels and hissing. Baby leapt to the other side, her fangs bared.

"Run!" yelled Roger. Leading the way he charged at the bogeybeast head on.

Kitty and Holly used the diversion to run past him. Holly dropped the lantern and it smashed into little pieces on the ground. They kept running and caught up with the red fireflies that had stopped to linger at the gateway to the library.

Racing toward home, Kitty scrambled over the back wall and dropped down into the garden, Holly right behind her. She fumbled in her pockets for the back door key, not wanting to look back in case the bogeybeast was there. The key twisted in the lock and the two friends tumbled through, landing in a pile on the floor.

Kitty jumped up and slammed the door shut, locking it and leaving the key in place. She hurried to her room and peeked out of the window, panting for breath, not sure what she would see.

The garden was empty and silent. No bogeybeast, which was good, but no cats either. "I hope they're OK."

Holly peered out from behind Kitty and into the garden. "Just us," she said.

"Seems so… How are the other gargoyles?" Kitty turned to look down at Holly.

"Gone." Holly's voice was barely more than a whisper.

"Gone? All of them?"

"Gone."

"What about the hunky punks, the others like you?"

"All gone. I'm the last." She stared down at her feet. "One by one they just disappeared. One minute they were there, the next, poof! That's why I came looking for you, I didn't know what else to do." Holly started to cry.

Kitty hugged her. "We'll find them and bring them back. I promise. In fact, I think I might know where they are."

Holly stopped crying and lifted her tear-streaked face. "Where?"

"Fairyland. That's where Mr. Wolf, the bogeyman, is taking Marcus and the Snodgrass family and my grandparents."

Remembering Mr. Wolf's threat to kidnap them, she dashed out of her room. "Grandma! Grandpa! Where are you?" She leapt up the stairs two at a time, Holly's stony feet clip-clopped up the stairs behind her.

Kitty burst into the kitchen to find it empty. Plates of food lay on the table with cups of half drunk tea. Kitty searched through the house, her tummy sinking with every empty room she passed. No one was home.

The house was as dark and empty as the garden outside.

She realized when she ran back into the kitchen that she heard only her own footsteps. "Holly?" She turned around to where Holly was standing just a moment ago. Only Holly wasn't there.

Holly had vanished.

Kitty was completely alone.

17 FAIRYLAND

KITTY RAN OUT of the front door, through the front gate and into Dr. McKracken's garden. "Dr. McKracken!" she called. There was no reply so she tried the handle of his back door. Finding it open, she dashed inside, calling out for the doctor. Her voice echoed through the empty house, he wasn't home.

Kitty's face creased with determination. With the Timekeeper in her hand, she ran back outside. Heading for the bottom of the garden, she was surprised when the door into Fairyland appeared, almost like it wanted her to find it quickly.

Baby and Nutmeg leapt over the wall and into her path.

"We chased that bogeybeast off!" said Nutmeg.

"What he means is, the bogeybeast ran away," said Baby. "He came in this direction, have you seen him?"

"No, but I know where to look." Kitty nodded toward the door to Fairyland.

"Where is Roger?" Kitty peered around.

Nutmeg and Baby glanced at each other and shook their heads.

"I hope he's OK." Not having time to brood over where

Roger might be, Kitty continued, "Look, I can't ask you to come with me, it's dangerous and—"

"Try and stop us!" said Nutmeg.

The three of them approached the door. Kitty in the middle with a cat hugging her shins on either side.

Taking a deep breath, Kitty pressed the button on top of the Timekeeper and together they stepped through into Fairyland.

The garden on the other side was a mess. Plants had been ripped up, their roots sticking helplessly into the air. Tattered petals and leaves covered the cobbled stones while the bee-like fairies buzzed frantically, whizzing over Kitty's head.

She could hear someone sobbing and followed the sound, stopping at a lump of rags at the foot of a tree.

The lump raised its head. It was the old hag. "Look at the mess! Look at it!" She waved her arm around.

Kitty felt sorry for the old hag and wanted to help her, but she needed to find her grandparents, Dr. McKracken and the Snodgrasses. "Who did this?"

"Him. The bogeyman. Him and his people dragged some poor souls this way."

She remembered what Beatrice Witcher had said about the old hag being a gatekeeper, and that the real Fairyland lay beyond these walls. Kitty steadied herself and in her most commanding voice said, "I need to enter Fairyland."

"You're in it," snapped the hag.

"No, I need to go beyond this gatehouse. I need to rescue the people the bogeyman brought here. I know you're the gatekeeper. I need to go into Fairyland right now!"

The old hag snorted. "For all the good it will do you." She waved her hand and the furthest wall of the garden vanished.

Kitty gasped in shock.

Beyond the gatehouse was a stinking, spooky bog with stunted black trees and spiky bog grass. Dark shapes flitted about. The smell was so bad that Kitty pulled her t-shirt over her nose. It didn't help.

"Not what you were expecting, is it?" The old hag's face broke into a wicked grin and she started to cackle. "Still going in?"

"Yes I am," Kitty said. She turned and marched toward the bog.

Passing the back wall of the gatehouse, her foot hit the ground with a sploosh. She shivered, she was up to her ankles in slimy water.

"Ugh!"

Goosebumps prickled Kitty's arms as she glanced around. It looked dead and dangerous. A crow squawked overhead. The smell here was even worse.

The cats picked their way through the bog, jumping from one patch of solid ground to the next. "Any idea where we're going?" asked Nutmeg.

Kitty sighed. She had no idea which direction to take but before she could tell the cats, a dark shadow fell across the ground. Her heart skipped a beat. She peered up to see an armored body with huge black leathery wings flap overhead. A long spiked tail steered the beast. A dragon. It swooped to the left, opened its jaws and breathed fire.

Kitty spotted a dark shape ahead. It came closer, and with a jolt she realized it was Marcus Snodgrass, and he was running for his life. She looked on in horror when Marcus screamed, flames shooting down around him, setting patches of bog grass alight. The dragon banked to the right and came back around to finish him off. Marcus ran, tripped over a stone and fell headlong into the chilly water with a splash.

The dragon bore down and set the surface of the water ablaze. There was no sign of Marcus. Kitty danced nervously on her toes but then she saw Marcus pop his head up in a patch of decaying reeds and crawl to a fire free bank, covered in slime and rotting leaves.

Up above the dragon circled around, searching for its prey, its long black tail swishing behind it. Unable to see him, the dragon screamed in frustration, a shrill sound that had Kitty covering her ears.

The dragon turned away, flying deeper into the bog giving Kitty her chance. She ran toward Marcus wading knee deep through the bog. Out of the corner of her eye, she saw shapes scuttle away into the mist. The cats picked their way across the ground at either side of her.

A hand rose up from the bog and grabbed her ankle.

She fell face down in a pile of reeds.

"Kitty! What are you doing here?" said Marcus. Dead leaves slid off his head.

"Looking for you and my grandparents, you idiot!"

"Sorry," Marcus let go of her leg. "I was just—"

Another scream rang out nearby.

"Emily!" Marcus recognized his sister's voice.

"This time, follow us. We can pick our way across the bog without getting sucked in," said Baby over her shoulder as the cats pounced their way toward the sound of Emily's shrill screams.

Both cats were clawing and hissing at a tree trunk when Kitty and Marcus caught up with them. Emily was half inside a hollow tree that had wrapped itself around her, its roots bound tightly around her legs.

"It looks like the tree is eating her," said Kitty.

Tendrils of bark fastened themselves ever tighter around

Emily. Kitty tried to pull at one, but another tendril wrapped itself around her hand. "It's got me now!"

More tentacles of bark whipped out and fastened around Marcus's foot, dragging him toward its mouth. "Now what?" He struggled against the tree.

"How should I know?" Kitty fought to free herself. "It seems like the more we resist the worse it gets."

"Things can't get any worse." Marcus yanked at the tree limb, but it pulled him in even further.

Emily screamed again.

He spoke too soon. Overhead a winged shadow passed over them followed by a screech of anger and a wave of fire, setting the people-eating tree ablaze.

The tree writhed its tendrils and shook its blackened trunk, trying to shake off the fire before releasing its grip. Marcus, Emily, and Kitty tried to struggle free. Being tangled among the lower limbs had protected them against the dragon's fiery breath.

Marcus broke free first, then Kitty. Together they pulled a stunned Emily from deep within the trunk. The tree thrashed and burned, groaning and creaking.

The dragon came around for another assault and then with a shriek it pulled out of its dive, hovering above them for a moment before flying off.

"That's weird," said Marcus. "I wonder what scared it... good for us though."

"Or not," said Kitty. "Whatever scared a dragon should scare us too."

"Agreed," said Baby from a patch of bog grass ahead of them.

"Let's keep moving," growled Nutmeg over his shoulder.

Kitty looked around warily and at first saw nothing but

swirling mist. As she squinted more closely, the mist formed into horned shapes, and those shapes were getting nearer.

"Run!"

All three of them ran from the misty creatures straight into a frightening monster. It rose up out of the bog, its body coated in slime and dead plants. Something pink and gooey was plastered to its straggly hair.

Emily and Marcus shrieked.

Kitty scowled and peered closer. "Mrs. Snodgrass?" she said, recognizing the pink pudding in her hair.

"I tripped and fell... oh my, what a mess..." said Mrs. Snodgrass examining herself.

"Ugh! You look disgusting," said Marcus.

"She's lost her mind, completely lost it," said Kitty, watching Mrs. Snodgrass pull moss out of her hair and smile at it.

Emily gaped with her mouth open like a fish.

"Well, you can have a family reunion later, right now we need to get out of here. I'll get you back to the gatehouse and then I'm going to look for my grandparents, I think they were brought here too," said Kitty.

"I haven't seen them," said Marcus.

"I'll find them," said Kitty.

The horned misty shapes rose out of the bog and flitted closer. Kitty watched them become denser, materializing into bones. Their skeletal forms hovered inches above the bog. They held longbows in their fleshless hands and Kitty gasped when an arrow skimmed by her ear.

"Run!" Kitty grabbed Emily and Mrs. Snodgrass, pulling them in the direction of the gatehouse. Marcus charged ahead of them.

Another arrow shot by, narrowly missing them but hitting

a small rodent. It seemed to deflate, like its bones had turned to mush inside its body. As they ran past it, Kitty saw its eyes flash in terror. It was still alive! Alive, paralyzed and with no bones. Kitty felt her heart pound in horror.

The group kicked up bog water and muck in their desperation to escape the skeletal archers. A splash of mud blinded Kitty and she winced, pulled to an abrupt stop by Marcus.

Before Kitty could yell at him, the Snodgrasses screamed.

Blinking away the grime, she covered her eyes against the blinding green light that had flared up in front of them. Looking over her shoulder she saw the bog creatures drifting away, back into the mist.

The light dimmed to a gentle green glow. Kitty opened her eyes and saw a beautiful woman dressed in shades of emerald, forest and sap green. Light shone all around her and tiny stars twinkled in her long brown hair.

"Who are you?" Kitty asked, awestruck by the woman in green.

"I am Mavis, the Fairy Queen," replied the woman with a smile.

Both cats brushed up against Kitty, their coats covered in mud and slime.

"Follow me," said the Fairy Queen. "Quickly now, the boglings scare away easily enough, but they will be back soon and their bog bolts are deadly."

"What are boglings and what do their bolts do?" asked Kitty.

From behind the Queen, a group of small men dressed in leaves with acorn hats appeared.

"The boglings are evil spirits of the bog. They lure the unwary off the path and into the Bog of Boredom where they shoot them with bog bolts," said the Fairy Queen, leading the way onto a narrow trail.

"They don't kill do they?" said Kitty, struggling to keep up with the Queen's graceful strides. The little oakmen hauled the Snodgrass family along behind her.

"Bog bolts suck out their victims bones, leaving them to die a slow and painful death. Fully conscious, but unable to move."

"That's horrible!" Kitty remembered the poor bog rodent she had seen, left alive but motionless except for its terrified eyes.

The bog quickly gave way to trees and in no time, they were in a green forest. Birds chirped and a blue spotted butterfly flew past Kitty's nose. Shafts of sunlight filtered through the branches leaving pools of golden light on the forest floor.

"My castle is not far," said the Fairy Queen. "You are lucky we found you. My oakmen were out on patrol when they spotted the boglings."

A squirrel scampered across a branch overhead and Kitty realized they had crossed some unseen threshold. Stepping into a clearing, Kitty marveled at a meadow of bluebells, each petal swaying gently in the breeze. At the far side of the clearing stood the strangest castle Kitty had ever seen.

"Welcome to my home," said the Fairy Queen, gesturing toward the castle. "You will be safe here, for now."

The bluebells felt soft against Kitty's legs as she headed for the castle. As they got closer, Kitty could see that the structure was not made not made of stone or brick, but of living trees that had grown into leafy turrets or twisted their branches like vines into walls. The four corners of the tree-castle soared into a brilliant blue sky.

At the Fairy Queen's approach, a living oak door swung open on gnarled wooden hinges. Kitty noticed the entryway creek and groan when they walked through. It was like the castle was talking.

They emerged into a sunlit courtyard filled with wild flowers and fruit trees of every kind. Bees buzzed lazily from flower to flower.

"Please, rest. My oakmen will bring your friends some refreshments and clean water to wash, then they will guide you all back to the gatehouse," the Fairy Queen said to Kitty. "But first, you and I must talk."

18 BOGLINGS

THE FAIRY QUEEN walked gracefully away, her robes rippling like sunshine upon waves.

Kitty followed with the cats at her heels, wincing when she realized she was leaving a trail of mud behind her. She was covered in muck, moss and slime.

The cats looked like they had been swimming in a sewer and smelled just as bad.

The Fairy Queen didn't seem to mind. She sat down upon a throne of living wood, draped with sparkling fabrics and cushions. Still alive, the tree was ancient, crooked and in full leaf. Branches twisted together between the trunks creating a seat big enough for two.

"Please, allow me to help you clean up." A gentle breeze tickled the leaves overhead and blew wafts of lavender and rose from the garden, blowing all trace of muck and stench from Kitty and the cats.

Kitty breathed deeply. The stinky bog with its fire-breathing dragons and man-eating trees, not to mention the cruel boglings, seemed a million miles away.

"Tea, Majesty." An oakman bowed, setting an earthy teapot and two goblets on a small table in front of them.

"Drink, this will revive and soothe you." The Queen filled both goblets and handed one to Kitty.

Lifting it to her lips, Kitty took a sip. It tasted of berries and lemon and warmed her throat.

Kitty sighed, her body relaxed and she felt as if she had just awoken from the best night's sleep ever. "This is wonderful!" She drained the goblet.

"Kitty Tweddle, you are in great danger." The Queen put down her goblet and clasped her hands together. "Our worlds are in great danger."

"You know who I am?"

"Of course. All in Fairyland know who you are, and what you can do. What you must do."

"What must I do?"

"Save us all."

"What, me? How? And where are my grandparents, I thought they were here—"

"Please listen very carefully." The Queen held up her hand. "There is little time. The bogeyman is attempting to bring his evil fairies into your world through the wishing well. For every bad fairy he brings into your world, he must send a human into Fairyland. I believe your companions are the first. As for your grandparents, they are not here, not yet."

Kitty nodded in understanding.

"But that's not all." The Queen looked grave. "Once he has gained enough strength, we believe he plans to take over your world and rule it."

"But why?"

"Power is a most seductive force, one a bogeyman can not resist. It is his nature to crave power over others," the Queen said with a sigh. "I know this is a tremendous burden, and the task seems great, but you have the power to stop him and his evil plan." The Queen smiled. "Kitty Tweddle, you are more powerful than you could possibly imagine."

Not knowing what to do, or even what to think, Kitty said, "OK."

"Take this." The Queen held out a golden coin. "This is a fairy coin, a lucky coin." She placed it in Kitty's outstretched hand. "In your darkest hour, when all seems lost, wish upon this penny."

Kitty held it up, sunlight glinted off its golden surface. An acorn adorned one side and the words, *Makes 1 Wish*, were inscribed on the reverse.

The Queen stood up. "My oakmen will guide you to the Sneaking Path. It will take you back to the gatehouse."

Feeling revived by the fairy tea, Kitty put the lucky coin in her pocket and together with the cats, followed the oakmen and the Snodgrasses toward the castle gate.

"Remember," the Queen called after them. "No matter what happens, do no stray into the Bog of Boredom, stay on the Sneaking Path!"

Once out of the gate and through the bluebell meadow, the oakmen pointed to the left fork in the road.

"Stay on the path," their leader said, echoing the Queen's words. Then the oakmen turned and disappeared into the trees.

"You heard the man," said Marcus, marching ahead.

Emily and Mrs. Snodgrass followed behind him leaving Kitty and the cats in the rear.

Baby looked worried.

Nutmeg scowled.

Kitty glanced from one to the other. "Let's keep moving."

They didn't get more than a few feet along the Sneaking Path when a shadow passed overhead.

It swerved toward them and fire incinerated the trees on either side.

The dragon was back.

"Stay on the path!" screamed Kitty. "Whatever you do, don't leave the path!"

Marcus yelled.

Emily screeched.

Kitty managed to grab onto Emily and Mrs. Snodgrass as the dragon bore down on them again. "Marcus!" she screamed, but it was too late. Marcus had already disappeared into the trees.

Mrs. Snodgrass chased after him, dragging Kitty and Emily along with her.

Kitty's breath rasped in her throat when she was pulled into the air and hung upside down in a bundle. They were caught in a rope trap!

Kitty could barely think for the sound of screaming in her ears. Someone's foot hit her face and through watering eyes, Kitty could see the boglings closing in around them. Bows raised and tipped with bone-mushing arrows.

There was nothing to be done, they would be fired upon and their bones turned to mush. Then, they would be left in a helpless heap like the poor bog rodent.

Her mind raced. They were hanging at least six feet above the ground. There was no way to escape.

The boglings glared up at them with sightless eyes and notched their deadly bog bolts.

Think!

The boglings pulled back their bows and took aim.

The Mantle, what if I hid us all inside a spell of invisibility?

Kitty thought. "Shhhh!" she hissed. "Be quiet! If they can't hear us, they can't shoot us," Kitty lied. She really needed to make them all disappear.

Kitty closed her eyes, ignoring the foot in her face and knee in her back and focused on The Mantle. In her mind's eye, she wrapped it around them all, cloaking them in invisibility.

Holding her breath, Kitty waited for the first bog bolt to strike. She imagined the horror of having her bones sucked out of her body, leaving her alive but completely helpless. She started to shiver and used all her strength to stop her teeth from chattering.

She opened one eye and risked a look down.

The boglings drifted around, searching for something that was there only a moment ago.

They can't see us anymore!

But they could still aim and shoot. Time for a distraction.

Although she could barely move inside the net, Kitty managed to poke one finger through it and point at the Bog of Boredom.

The water plopped.

Then splooshed.

The boglings turned in the direction of the sound.

Kitty focused every last scrap of concentration, screwed up her face, wrinkled her nose, and made the water boil.

Their bows had gone slack and were pointed down. They bumped into each other as they drifted away.

It worked!

Kitty heard a rasping, gnawing sound. Baby, who was at the top of the pile, had already started to gnaw at the rope holding them up. Nutmeg wrestled his way through their pile of limbs to join her and together they chewed through.

Splat!

They fell to the soft boggy ground in a painful heap.

"Ouch!"

"Get your foot out of my face!" yelled Kitty.

"Not my fault!" Marcus barked and rolled away.

Emily just sobbed and Mrs. Snodgrass stared at her hands like she had never seen them before.

Marcus grumbled and stood up. "Now what?" He looked at Kitty.

"Help your mother and sister up for a start."

Mrs. Snodgrass lay on her back with her feet in the air like a beetle. Her clothes and hair were covered in rotting leaves and her face was green with bog slime. She held out a gooey hand to her son. "Help me up Marcus, there's a good boy," she said.

Marcus grimaced and grabbed her wrist, avoiding the goo, and pulled her to her feet. She tottered almost losing her balance forcing Marcus to help steady her.

Emily scrambled to her feet and clung to her mother's arm, still silent, her mouth wide open in shock.

Kitty glanced around. They had been on their way back to the gatehouse when the boglings attacked and it was right... She turned on the spot, scanning the view in all directions, but there was no sign of the path or the gatehouse.

They were lost.

Nutmeg stood up on his hind legs trying to get a better view. Baby climbed up a straggly tree and twisted around.

"Do you see the gatehouse?" asked Kitty.

Both cats shook their heads before trotting over to Kitty, rubbing themselves against her legs for comfort.

"What do we do now, Kitty?" asked a quiet voice.

Kitty turned around. It belonged to Emily, only it didn't

sound like her at all. There was no teasing, no shrieking, demanding or pleading. She just sounded scared.

Kitty was scared too, although she couldn't show it. Right now, they were all depending on her to get them safely away from here. Away from Fairyland and its boglings with their bog bolts, slimy mud pits, fire-breathing dragons and people-eating trees.

They all stared at her and waited.

"Now we go home." Kitty reached for the Timekeeper hanging around her neck.

"Do you think the Heart Stone will lead us back to the gatehouse?" asked Baby.

The Snodgrasses did not hear, of course, to them Baby just said, *meow*.

"Lets see," Kitty said, popping the Timekeeper open. She held the Heart Stone in her hand, closed her eyes and thought of her grandparents' home, hoping with all her heart that it would work.

She opened her eyes to a swarm of red fireflies rising from the Heart Stone. They danced around in a circle before sparkling over the clumps of bog grass and twisting away to the left. Kitty's shoulders sagged in relief. "This way!" she said, running after the fireflies. The cats leaped ahead while the Snodgrasses shambled behind.

The fireflies led them to the Sneaking Path, completely hidden from view until they were on top of it.

The glowing red lights twisted and spiraled down the Sneaking Path, leading them through the bog.

"Look," said Marcus. The mists shifted ahead of them. "I can see the gatehouse." He pointed, grinning from ear to ear with relief at the red brick walls.

The little group picked up their pace, relieved to be on

their way home. They ran into the gatehouse garden, still in a shambles with flowers and leaves thrown everywhere.

"You're back?"

Kitty noticed the surprise in the old hag's voice. "Yes, and now we're going home."

"That's what you think," the old hag spat. She pulled herself to her feet, leaning heavily on a makeshift staff fashioned from a broken tree branch. She hobbled up to Kitty, screwed up her face and repeated, "That's what you think!"

"The old bat already said that, she's obviously mad," said Marcus, marching toward the doorway to Dr. McKracken's back garden and the real world. Emily and Mrs. Snodgrass hurried to keep up with him.

The old hag turned to watch him. "You'll see..."

Kitty shook her head. Sick of the old hag's games, she caught up with the Snodgrass family. With Marcus to her left and Emily to her right she said, "Marcus, Emily, grab my arm, Mrs. Snodgrass, hold onto Marcus." The cats slid in either side of her legs. "We all go through together."

She held the Timekeeper and pushed the door.

It didn't move.

She pushed again, kicking and throwing her weight against the wood. The door remained closed.

"We're stuck here," wailed Emily.

"Ha! Told you!" The old hag started to cackle and the leaves on the top of her staff quivered.

"What's going on? Why can't we go through?" Kitty demanded.

"Your friends here can't get out till them three that left comes back."

"So I can go alone?"

"You and your cat friends, yes, but not them." She glared at the Snodgrass family. "They have to stay."

"I want to go home," Emily sobbed.

"Let us out of here this instant, you old hag!" shouted Marcus.

"Wait here," said Kitty, "I'm going to find out what's going on. Don't move." She strode toward the door to the star room with the cats at her heels.

To her relief, the star room was exactly as she had left it. The Seeingscope pointed up to a starry sky, charts covered the walls and books littered the old wooden desks.

Kitty formed the question in her mind—*how can we all get home?* She put her eye up against the lens and looked through for her answer.

Leavers cranked and wheels turned bringing the Seeingscope to life. It belched steam from a brass funnel while blue and yellow lights sparkled and swirled around her.

She sighed. The cats wandered in figure eights around her ankles. "Well, if that's the only way, then that's what I'll do."

"Do what?" asked Nutmeg.

"Leave them here."

"You can't," said Baby.

"Just for now." Kitty crouched down to face Baby. "The old hag was telling the truth, the Snodgrasses can't go back until those who left Fairyland return."

"So what are we going to do?" said Nutmeg.

"We're going to find the bad fairies and send them back," said Kitty. "And I think I know how. Come on."

She walked back across the courtyard to the Snodgrasses who were still standing next to the door. She took a deep breath and said, "I need to catch your kidnappers and bring them back here before you can leave."

All three Snodgrasses stared at her.

"You can't just leave us here," growled Marcus.

"I'm sorry, there's no other way. Stay close to the doorway, really close. And don't move no matter what happens. I'll be back, I promise."

Without another word, Kitty and the cats stepped through the doorway and into Dr. McKracken's garden.

19 THE AXE

KITTY LEFT a trail of muddy footprints on the garden path. Her strides were long, keeping her attention on the back door of number five Crescent Avenue. She stopped so suddenly that Nutmeg, who had been trotting behind, ran into her legs.

"Ouch! Why are we stopping?" he said.

"Dr. McKracken?" Kitty bent down over his crumpled form. He held a hand to his head, and beneath his fingers Kitty could see a large purple bump. Helping him to sit up Kitty asked, "What happened?"

"Monsters. Big Monsters." He clutched his head and squeezed is eyes tight shut in pain. "I'll be alright, just give me a minute…"

"Don't move, I'll get help," said Kitty, not entirely sure where she was going to get any help from. The Snodgrass family were trapped in Fairyland and her grandparents had disappeared.

"Look," said Baby. She had trotted ahead and was almost at the house. "The back door, it's open."

Kitty left Dr. McKracken's side and crept closer. Nutmeg stood beside Baby, his ears pricked toward the house. The sound of breaking glass made them all jump. Then a small figure skittered across the dim passageway.

"Someone's inside," whispered Kitty.

"Burglars?" asked Nutmeg.

A heavy thud sounded from the basement followed by a chorus of nasty laughter.

"Not burglars," hissed Baby, her teeth bared.

"Night stealers," said Nutmeg with a deep sigh.

A scream echoed from within the house.

"Grandma!" Kitty ran into the basement, slipped and fell flat on her back.

She tried to get up when a hairy foot stomped on her chest, knocking the breath out of her. She looked up into the face of an ugly night stealer. It wore a crazed grin and something stinky dripped from its body. It smelled like compost.

More night stealers leaned in, lots of them, crowding over her.

A cat yowled and they scattered.

THWUMP!

A hissing Nutmeg landed on top of her. Kitty could hear Baby hissing and snarling, sending the night stealers scurrying in all directions.

Nutmeg turned around on Kitty's chest and looked down at her face. "Are you alright?"

"Yes," she croaked. "Do you mind?"

"Oh, sorry." He jumped to the floor and picked his way through the sea of dirt while Kitty struggled to her feet.

"What's the plan?" yelled Baby.

Kitty glanced around. The night stealers were covered in potting soil and stinky compost. They had emptied every packet, jar and bag in the little gardening supply cupboard and rolled around in it. One of them wore a purple gardening glove on his head. Another two fenced with trowels. They ran from room to room chased by both cats, screaming and laughing like this was the best game ever. The place was a complete mess. Kitty could barely think above the racket.

"Kitty!" Grandma called out. Her grandmother stood struggling between two monstrous figures and Kitty froze, watching in horror as they pushed her grandmother into the forbidden room at the end of the passageway.

One of the hunched forms turned and leered at Kitty. She recognized the three pot bellied trolls she had encountered after escaping the crypt. They were most likely brought from Fairyland by Mr. Wolf in exchange for the Snodgrass family.

One look at her Grandma's terrified face and Kitty was running down the passageway. She jumped over at least two night stealers and shoved another one out of the way.

Both cats bounded along behind her with their ears pinned back and fangs bared, ready to fight.

She reached the forbidden room and burst through the door.

The wishing well had grown in size and was now taller than Kitty. Mr. Wolf stood behind it with two trolls, whispering strange words at her grandparents. They appeared spellbound.

"Welcome Kitty," Mr. Wolf sneered, his bewitchment of Kitty's grandparents complete. "Well, well, what a lovely family reunion this is." He squeezed her Grandma's shoulder, making her face wrinkle in pain.

"Get off my Grandma right now!"

"Or what?" His cronies sniggered. "What are you and your little cat friends going to do about it?"

Nutmeg and Baby hissed.

"I... I'm not going to let you get away with this!" Kitty stammered. She had no idea what she could do about it. It was just her and the cats against Mr. Wolf and his trolls, and a powerful rogue wishing well full of wicked wishes.

Kitty's skin crawled at the cold malice in Mr. Wolf's eyes. He barked a laugh, the sound rough and inhuman.

Kitty's grandparents stood very still appearing rather confused. *Why don't they do anything? Why don't they fight?*

"Grandma? Grandpa? What's wrong? Don't stand there— do something!"

"They can't do anything," said Mr. Wolf. "They are completely under my power, as you will be very soon." He grinned from ear to ear showing his long canines. His cronies grunted.

"To start with, I will draw every nasty, wicked and unpleasant wish out of this wishing well and make them all come true here and now." He started to walk around the wishing well to face Kitty. "But that's just the beginning."

Something tugged inside Kitty's brain. Mr. Wolf was making powerful threats, but he hadn't done anything yet. What was he waiting for? "Then why haven't you? If you're so powerful," she blurted out. "Why haven't you done it yet?" Kitty was amazed at how confident she sounded, she really didn't feel it, but something else had taken over her, a part of her she didn't even know she had.

"I believe you have already had a taste of what those wishes are like? You have picked up a few bad pennies yourself, am I right?"

Kitty edged away from him, backing toward the door.

He plunged his hand into the well and pulled out an old penny. "I wonder what wish was made with this one?" He flipped the penny into the air. It glinted, twisted and fell back into his palm. "It won't work on me of course, as a creature of Fairyland I am immune." He held it out to Kitty. "Would *you* like to pick it up and see?"

Kitty shook her head and stepped back. "No."

She remembered the first penny she had picked up. The wish from that coin had covered her face in boils while the second had left her with ridiculous hair. While those had been fairly harmless, the coin Grandpa picked up had turned him into a scarecrow, and Kitty had used up the last of the antidote to wishes changing him back.

"As soon as the wishing well is complete—and it will be momentarily—you will regret your insolence!"

Kitty scanned the wishing well, quickly taking note of everything, the base, the roof, the little tiles, the handle used to lower the bucket... but no bucket!

Mr. Wolf must have seen the flash of understanding in her eyes. "Yes, the bucket, and you know exactly where it is, don't you?"

Kitty shook her head, "No way am I helping you."

"Oh, but you will. Or I'll kill your grandparents." Mr. Wolf pulled out a wicked looking knife and held it against Grandma's neck.

"No!" Kitty's breath rasped in her throat. "No, please don't hurt my grandparents, I'll tell you what you want to know." She gulped hard. She didn't want to tell Mr. Wolf anything, but she couldn't let him hurt her Grandma.

"If I tell you where it is, you won't hurt my grandparents?"

"You have my word."

Sighing in defeat, Kitty's head dropped. "Upstairs in the living room cupboard next to the fireplace."

"I knew it would be close. I suspected within the walls of this very home. It will most likely be old and rusty, but that doesn't matter. It's a magical item, it's the magic that matters. Only the magic matters."

Kitty tried to run for the main stairs, but one of the trolls blocked her path, his massive arms crossed while his beady eyes goggled down at her with amusement. Remembering that the bucket was in a cupboard connected to the secret passageways, Kitty fled in the other direction, back down the passageway toward her bedroom.

"Go and get Dr. McKracken!" she yelled to the cats. "We're going to need some help." The cats ran out of the back door while Kitty raced into her room and pulled the door to the secret passageways open.

She didn't have time to light a candle, but she only needed to get up one floor. Leaving the entrance door open to let enough light filter through, she leaped up the stairs two at a time. Stumbling a little, she reached the top but she was going so fast she couldn't stop and burst through the little secret door and into the cupboard. Straight into the arms of one of Mr. Wolf's trolls.

"Gotcha!" The brute picked her up with one hand, tossing her over his shoulder like a sack of grain and carried her out of the room.

"Get off me!" Kitty screamed and kicked with all her strength. It made no difference. She could see the bucket in his hand. Once that bucket was attached to the wishing well, all would be lost. There would be nothing Kitty could do to save the Snodgrasses, her grandparents or herself.

Kitty hung her head. What could she do? Her grandparents were bewitched by Mr. Wolf, Dr. McKracken was injured and she had sent the cats away. And, she had failed to get the magic bucket.

Was there any hope? If there was, Kitty couldn't see it.

She had trouble breathing as she was roughly carried down the stairs and back to the forbidden room. When she was set down, she was so dizzy that her head started to spin and she almost fell over.

"Nice try," said Mr. Wolf. "I think we'll skip the preliminary bad wishes and go straight to my big wish." He held up the bucket. "Something I have been wishing to happen for a very long time. You have no idea how many bad pennies I have thrown into wishing wells over the years, each with an ardent wish for a whole world to rule over. Now, let's see what happens when I attach the bucket to the wishing well."

Kitty tried once more to wrestle free of the troll, but he held her fast.

"You know, it took me a long time to find this handle. That witch, Beatrice, wouldn't tell me where it was. So I killed her."

Kitty gasped, "Grandpa said she disappeared. But it was you all along, you murdered her."

"Yes, and began years and years of fruitless searching. Do you know where this handle was? In the crypt under the library. Why else would I take this human form and work as a friendly librarian? To give me access to the crypt and search it for this magical device." He attached the bucket to the wishing well.

At first Kitty thought she was still dizzy from being carried upside down, but she realized that something was swirling in the room.

The walls seemed to be... disappearing. She tried to focus on what lay beyond.

"No!" she cried out with horror.

"Oh yes," said Mr. Wolf, his face alight with glee. "You know what's coming, you know what I've wished for don't you, Kitty Tweddle? And I have to say, without your help, none of this would have been possible."

"What? What are you talking about? I didn't help you. I would never help you!"

"Not intentionally I admit, but your presence, your magical presence has made all of this so much easier."

Kitty's brow creased. "What do you mean?"

"Magic seeps in through the cracks. Your world, your reality, is not as solid as it seems. There are places where little bits of magic collect. I've been collecting bits of magic for some time now and directing them here, to this wishing well. It would have taken me a good deal longer, perhaps years. Then you came, Kitty Tweddle, a being filled with magic, you moved into this house! I couldn't believe my good fortune. Your magical presence and the magic that seeps from you have brought my plans to glorious fruition far earlier than I ever dreamed. So you see, you have helped me and for that I thank you."

Kitty couldn't bear to look at his smug face and turned away.

"Of course, those troublesome gargoyles had to be removed. One by one I picked them off every building and made them disappear. And to be sure, I hid every hunky punk too. What makes this all so very satisfying, is that I did this using your magic!" He laughed.

The walls of the room crumbled, and the one place she never wanted to see again began forming all around her.

The bog from Fairyland.

The misty gloom, people eating trees, spiky bog grass and evil boglings armed with deadly bog bolts, all hovered at the edges of the room. While the walls continued to fall down all around her, the Bog of Boredom came nearer and nearer.

"Now, it's time for the world as you know it to end." He turned the handle and began lowering the bucket. "Your world will become one big Bog of Boredom, and I will rule over it all!"

At first, wisps of smoke came off the water, but those wisps soon took the form of ghostly skeletons dressed in rags. They floated up toward the ceiling, more and more of them came pouring out of the wishing well.

Kitty's heart was pounding. Her grandparents stood before her in the clutches of Mr. Wolf—bewitched like statues. She struggled against her captor. He held tight, hurting her arms.

She looked down. The huge troll had a hole in his boot where his big toe poked through. Without thinking, Kitty raised her foot and stamped down as hard as she could.

He yelped and let go just enough for her to wriggle one arm free.

One of the misty skeletons brushed against her hand, its touch was cold as ice. Kitty plunged her hand into her pocket out of instinct, to warm it. Once in her pocket, her fingers found a small metal object there. Something she had forgotten about. Something the fairy Queen had given her when she was in Fairyland.

The lucky penny.

Kitty remembered the Fairy Queen's words.

In your darkest hour, when all seems lost, wish upon this penny.

The lucky penny glinted in her hand as Kitty pulled it from her pocket. But what could she wish for? To stop this madness? To make Mr. Wolf go back to where he came from? What she really needed right now was some help.

"What is that? What are you looking at?" Mr. Wolf's face screwed up. He turned to the trolls. "What's in her hand?" His eyes widened. "Get it!"

Before the troll holding her could react, Kitty threw the coin into the well. "I wish for help to come out of this wishing well!"

Mr. Wolf and his cronies all tried to grab for the penny at the same time, getting in each other's way. The penny made it through their outstretched fingers toward the water below.

PLINK-PLINK-PLINK.

It ricocheted off the inner walls of the wishing well.

SPLOOSH!

Kitty realized she was holding her breath. The seconds ticked by and she let it out with a deep sigh.

Nothing happened.

Mr. Wolf began to laugh.

Kitty began to cry.

She didn't want to. She tried her very hardest not to. But she had never felt so hopeless in her entire life. While the tears were trickling down her cheeks and her nose bunged up, she heard it. It was a whirring sound at first, but then it got louder and louder.

Mr. Wolf stopped laughing, his forehead creasing in worry.

The whirring became a flapping. Something was coming out of the wishing well.

A blast of wings and talons burst out, filling the room with a thunderous sound and creating quite a draft.

There were so many of them Kitty couldn't make out what they were at first. Their winged forms swarmed, forcing Mr. Wolf and his trolls to duck. They flew straight through the skeleton things that vanished with a *hiss*.

Kitty ducked behind the wishing well.

"No!" shrieked Mr. Wolf.

Kitty peeped out and then realized what the flying creatures were.

Gargoyles.

Her wish had come true, some help had come out of the wishing well.

Each of the gargoyles found a perch. They covered the well, the shelves, the furniture and even the heads of Mr. Wolf's cronies.

All at once they opened their mouths and began to sing.

A troop of night stealers skipped into the forbidden room, shrieking with laughter and throwing food at each other, completely unaware of the singing gargoyles.

The most beautiful music filled the room, transfixing the night stealers who stood spellbound.

The walls of the room started rebuilding themselves. The Fairyland bog faded into golden light. Although she didn't know how, Kitty felt the golden light had something to do with the gargoyle-song.

"No! I will not be beaten, not now, not after all I have done." Mr. Wolf let go of Kitty's grandparents and started to lower the bucket into the well. "It's too late for the gargoyles to help you now!"

Grandpa fell back against the wall and snapped out of Mr. Wolf's spell, catching Grandma before she fell.

"Grandpa? Are you awake?" Kitty ran to help him.

Suddenly, a black furry blur shot in front of Kitty's face, over the wishing well and attached itself to Mr. Wolf's arm.

Mr. Wolf howled in pain when fangs sunk deep into his flesh and claws ripped at his face and body. His arms flailed, trying to pull his attacker off.

He screamed for his trolls to do something, but they

huddled on the floor with their hands over their ears, unable to bare the gargoyle-song.

It took Kitty a moment to recognize the black ball of fur attacking Mr. Wolf.

"Roger!"

Kitty knew she had to act fast.

She stepped backward until she felt the door frame and then turned, took a step out of the room and came face to face the with the axe.

The axe had frightened her when she first came to number five Crescent Avenue. She had avoided it every time she had walked past. But now, she smiled and reached for it.

The handle felt warm to the touch, as if it were alive. Light glinted off its curved edge like a wicked grin when she lifted it off the hook. Surprised at how light it was, Kitty adjusted her grip.

Holding the axe felt good. Like she was meant to wield it. As if it *wanted* her to unleash its power.

Kitty walked back into the forbidden room. Raising the axe above her head, her brow creased with determination, she brought it down hard, smashing the roof of the wishing well. Little red tiles flew everywhere.

Mr. Wolf screamed.

The gargoyle-song soared.

Roger yowled.

She swung the axe again, light as a feather but sure as an arrow it hit its mark, destroying the base of the wishing well, splintering its wooden sides into toothpicks.

Kitty felt like she was dancing and the axe was taking the lead. It *knew* what to do.

The golden light of the gargoyle-song lit up the room like a fire, filling it with goodness.

She lifted the axe one more time. Arching her body, she brought it down low, chopping the wishing well off at ground level with one sure swish of the blade.

Only a huge round water-filled hole remained in the floor.

It began to swirl, like water down a plughole. One after the other, the three trolls were sucked in, head first.

Mr. Wolf struggled with Roger, trying to fight him off. Covered in blood, he staggered forward and was sucked into the well, taking Roger with him.

"Roger! No!" Kitty screamed. Dropping the axe she plunged her hands into the swirling water, but she felt nothing.

"Roger? Roger where are you?" She was up to her armpits, reaching as far as she could, desperately trying to grab onto Roger's furry body, but there was nothing there.

Roger was gone.

"Come along dear, they're gone," Grandpa said gently.

Kitty gazed into her Grandpa's kind face through tear-streaked eyes. "Oh, Grandpa!"

She looked around the room. Water swirled down the well, sucking in all of the splintered wood.

In a few moments, it stopped and the room was back to the way it was before. The walls, the furniture, the shelves stacked with bottles of wine, everything just looked... normal.

Mr. Wolf and his trolls were gone.

The gargoyles hopped down from their perches and busied themselves rounding up the night stealers, singing a soft lullaby to coax them away. One by one, they padded down the passageway and into the garden.

Zebulon and Holly the hunky punk were the last to leave.

"Well done, Kitty Tweddle." Zebulon nodded.

Holly grabbed her for a quick hug before trotting off after Zebulon.

The gargoyles' stony paws left no sign of their passing.

When they had all gone, Baby and Nutmeg came galloping toward her, followed by a slightly dazed Dr. McKracken and a very muddy Snodgrass family.

20 AN UNEXPECTED FRIEND

A FLURRY of orange leaves dropped from the branches of the old plum tree, landing on the lawn of number five Crescent Avenue. A crisp wind swirled them across the grass until they piled around the feet of a statue of a bathing lady. An apple dropped to the ground with a thud. Autumn came early to the village of Dribble.

The breeze ruffled the curtains at Kitty's bedroom window. On the floor, the book of magic lay open and a purple door, about three feet tall, popped out of it.

Munin snored, perched on Kitty's shoulder, his head tucked under his mechanical wing. She sat in Munin's endless library at a huge wooden desk, piled high with books, scrolls, and Crystalizers.

Since she had destroyed the wishing well and banished the bogeyman back to Fairyland, Kitty had spent all her free time studying magic. It kept her mind off Roger, the stray black cat who had saved her life and the whole world, sacrificing himself in the process.

Magic, it turned out, wasn't exactly what she had expected.

Kitty had always imagined magic to be spells, sparkles, potions, pointy hats with stars on and lots of witchy jewelry.

Well, there were potions. Lots of them. Mostly to cure ailments—everything from sore throats to bee stings using herbs from the garden.

There were spells of a kind. But nothing that went boom and definitely no sparkles. Not for novice witches. Except on special occasions.

Magic for beginners, Kitty learned, was about mastering the thoughts in her head, which in turn controlled the words that come out of her mouth and the actions that tended to come along for the ride. It was all so very... practical.

Beatrice walked up to the desk and Munin fluttered to her shoulder. "I do believe this book is due back at the library."

"Cor!"

"I know." Kitty sighed. "There is just so much to learn..." She waved her hand at the unending shelves of magical knowledge, everything Beatrice had collected over her lifetime.

"Which root would you make into a tea for travel sickness?" Beatrice asked.

"Ginger."

"Name the most effective treatment for toenail fungus."

"Oil of oregano."

"Name three herbs that are good for your skin."

"Calendula, comfrey and lavender."

"Name the three most important things that a witch must be."

Kitty thought about it for a moment. "Fearless, determined and... practical."

Beatrice walked around the desk and hugged her. Munin rubbed his metal head against hers. "Well, you've got the basics. Now, it's time to go."

Munin squawked and flew into the depths of his library.

Beatrice walked with Kitty back into the cottage leaving her at the front door.

"Will I ever see you again?" Kitty asked.

Beatrice smiled. "There were a few copies of this book published, they are all enchanted. Each one is a portal to this cottage. I am sure of it."

Kitty took one last look around the witch's cottage before crawling out of the purple door on all fours and back into her bedroom.

Kitty sat down at the kitchen table. Behind her the kettle whistled to a boil and the radio blared out the news. "The city's gargoyles return! Although no one knows where they went, who took them or why, we can report that all gargoyles reported missing over the summer have been returned."

"Well, that's good news isn't it?" said Grandma. Not waiting for a reply, she turned the volume down and filled the teapot. "There, now." She put a knitted tea cozy on the pot like a hat and brought it over to the table.

Kitty helped herself to a slice of toast and although she couldn't see Grandpa behind his paper, Kitty knew he was happy about the gargoyles returning too.

"What are your plans for your last day with us?" he asked.

"Well," Kitty said through a mouthful of toast. "I have a book to return to the library and then I need to say goodbye to some friends."

Grandma poured tea into three china teacups. "That's nice dear. Is your suitcase packed?"

"Yes."

After breakfast, Kitty picked up the book of magic from her bedroom floor and set out for the library. Since Mr. Wolf, the bogeyman, had disappeared, Mrs. Snodgrass had been promoted to head librarian, which suited her. She was known to be very strict about book returns.

Kitty walked up the library steps and pushed open the door. How strange it looks in daylight, she thought walking up to the returns desk.

"Returning a book?" asked a helpful young librarian.

"Um, yes." Kitty handed over the musty copy of How to be Witchy: Practical Magic for Everyday Enchantment.

The librarian scanned the book and looked confused. "This doesn't appear to have been scanned out."

"Oh?"

"Hmm, scanners must have been down again," she said.

Kitty said nothing and tried to act natural.

"Well, thank you for returning the book, anything else I can help you with?"

"No, that's all, thanks."

She turned and walked out of the library feeling quite sad. She really wanted to keep the book. What if she needed to talk to Beatrice Witcher again? But the book wasn't hers to keep. She knew that returning it was the right thing to do.

Her thoughts drifted back to Roger.

Nutmeg and Baby were waiting at the library steps.

"Hello," Kitty said.

"Why so sad?" asked Baby.

"I just keep thinking about Roger, stuck in that horrible Fairyland bog."

"Roger is a stray cat, he knows how to look after himself," said Baby quickly.

Nutmeg looked up at the sky.

Kitty sighed, "I know you're trying to make me feel better, thanks."

Baby and Nutmeg exchanged knowing glances.

"You're leaving today, aren't you?" asked Baby changing the subject.

"Yes, I am."

"We'll miss you." Nutmeg glanced away.

Kitty sat down on the stone steps and hugged them both.

"Well, I'm not saying goodbye." Nutmeg snorted.

"We'll see you soon." Baby brushed against her.

"That feels a lot better," said Kitty. She looked back at the library, at the stone steps and the big wooden door. She smiled at the two gargoyles stationed at each side of the entrance, exactly where they should be.

"What about—"

"The night stealers are sleeping in the crypt, the gargoyles have them completely safe and under control, you don't have to worry," said Baby.

"Go on then, we know you have other people to see before your train leaves this afternoon," said Nutmeg. "See you!" And with that, he bounded away.

"He's very emotional you know, even though he tries to hide it," said Baby.

"I know."

Baby rubbed her face against Kitty's hand, then gently raised her head so that they were eye to eye. "Take good care of yourself, Kitty Tweddle."

Kitty hurried back to the house. She arrived to see Grandpa heaving her bags to the front door.

"We were wondering where you had got to," he said.

"Now are you sure you have everything packed?" Grandma asked.

"Yes, I'm sure."

The taxi pulled up at the front door with two sharp peeps of his horn.

Kitty walked down the garden path with her grandparents behind her.

Dr. McKracken was standing by the front gate. "You've still got the... You know." He patted his chest.

"Safe and sound." Kitty patted the Timekeeper that she wore around her neck. Then she hugged him. "I'll miss you."

"Oh, none of that now!" he said with a sniff. "You will be coming back soon, won't you?"

"Yes I will." She looked around at the faces of Dr. McKracken and her grandparents. "I will be back soon."

"Kitty! Kitty! Wait!" Emily Snodgrass ran out of her front door and along the garden path in her bare feet. "I got you this." She thrust out a necklace. It was oddly fashioned out of gaudy plastic beads with glittery bits in them. "I made it myself," she said proudly.

Mrs. Snodgrass appeared at Emily's side looking haughty as ever. She patted her daughter's shoulder. "That was very kind of Emily. Wasn't it?" She looked sternly at Kitty.

"Thank you Emily, that was very kind," said Kitty.

Peeking past Emily and Mrs. Snodgrass, Kitty could see Marcus scowling by the front door.

"Best be getting in the taxi," said Grandpa.

The taxi driver opened the door for her and put her bags inside.

After hugging her grandparents one last time, Kitty clambered in and put on her seatbelt. A moment later the taxi pulled away. She waved to everyone until the taxi turned the corner onto Hornblower Street and she couldn't see them anymore.

Sighing, she turned to face the front. That's when she noticed one of her bags moving. It jumped to the left, grunted, then jumped to the right.

She leaned forward and unzipped it.

"Finally!" said Roger as he pulled himself out of the bag.

"Roger! How? I mean I thought you got sucked into the well!" Kitty couldn't believe it.

"I did, and then I got spat back out again. After you lot had left the room. All wet and with bits of wood in my fur. Took me forever to get all those splinters out I can tell you and—"

"Oh, Roger!" Kitty picked him up and hugged him.

Roger grimaced.

"What's wrong?" she asked.

"Well," he said, looking embarrassed, "I've just never been hugged before."

Kitty beamed. "What were you doing in my bag?"

"Well, you see, um, I've been a stray all my life. Love my freedom and all that, but, well, the thing is..." He started turning in circles on the seat next to her. "I'm kind of thinking it might be nice to be somebody's cat. Baby has her human people and Nutmeg has his and they take care of them, feed them, play with them, give them hugs..." He looked at her with big eyes.

Kitty just stared at him.

"I understand that having a human is a huge responsibility," he continued. "You have to curl up on their laps and sleep, wake them up in the morning, round up and store small items they may have lost under the sofa for safe keeping and nibble their hands from time to time. I've given it a great deal of thought and I've decided, I am ready for a human of my own!"

"You have?"

"I chose you!" Roger sat with his chest puffed out, trying to look his very best.

Kitty's mouth fell open.

Roger's happy grin slid and he looked down. "Well, of course, you might not want a cat like me, I mean—"

"Yes! I'd love that. I mean, I do, I do want a cat like you!" Kitty grinned from ear to ear and hugged Roger again.

The taxi sped on through the cobbled streets, passing dark alleyways and old churches on route to the train station.

All beneath the watchful gaze of the city's gargoyles.

Thank you for reading. I hope you have enjoyed Kitty Tweddle and the Wishing Well and I invite you to share your thoughts and reactions on:

Amazon and Goodreads

If you would like to know more about Kitty Tweddle, please visit the website: hjblenkinsop.com

For more of Kitty Tweddle's adventures, look out for these titles, coming soon:

Kitty Tweddle and the Secrets of Smugglers Cove

Kitty Tweddle and the Changelings of Witchway

ABOUT THE AUTHOR

H.J. Blenkinsop lives the wilds of New York with her family which includes a three-legged cat called Miracle. When she's not cooking up strange tales, H.J. dabbles in soap making and potion mixing.